Fontana African Novels

Many Thing Begin for Change

Adaora Lily Ulasi

Fontana/Collins

Humorous confrontations between
White officials and black tribes-
men in Ukana, a village of Nigeria.

First published in Great Britain by
Michael Joseph Ltd 1971
First issued in Fontana Books 1975

© 1971 by Adaora Lily Ulasi

Made and printed in Great Britain by
William Collins Sons & Co Ltd Glasgow

Chapter One

The District Officer, Maurice Mason, a dark-haired rotund man in his forties, of medium height, stood disbelieving one minute, and pleading for his life to be spared in the next, when the axe finally fell across his neck and a well sharpened machete neatly severed his head from the rest of his body on this Monday morning in Ukana.

In the space of an hour, neither his assassins nor any trace of what had just taken place was visible. The clearing, where a man had just been murdered, and which had been teeming with people, was suddenly deserted save for the newly turned earth carefully concealed with dry leaves. And in the years to come this time and place would be nothing but a neat patch of barren land – except to the assassins.

In Utuka, the region's headquarters, the inhabitants had also been astir and about their various business. Some could be found in the market place with their wares; others in shops; and more in the river fishing or up to the palm tree tapping the wine.

But in the government offices, Jack Bailey, a young man with a round face topped by blond hair, dressed in white shorts and shirt, and recently appointed as junior secretary to the Regional Government, leaned his elbows on the window of the District Office as he waited for the District Officer, Maurice Mason, to arrive.

The scene that spread itself before Bailey was one which he had seen every day since he took up his appointment three months ago. He screwed up his pale blue eyes against the blinding sun from a cloudless African sky, as he stared at the township of Utuka.

The phone rang. Bailey picked it up. 'Yes?'

'Please hold the line for the District Commissioner,' said the telephone operator.

The voice of George Hughes came on the line. He was an able but gruff administrator of medium build and height with a pair of hazel eyes and a cultivated moustache.

'Maurice,' he rasped out, 'haven't you any idea what the time is? Shouldn't you be in court – ?'

Bailey spoke up. 'This is Jack Bailey, sir.'

'Who? Oh! Let me speak to Maurice will you?' said Hughes impatiently.

'He isn't here. I mean, he hasn't come in yet.'

Hughes looked at his watch. It said nine-thirty. 'Hmm,' he grunted. 'Is he still at home then?'

When Bailey replied that he didn't know, Hughes grunted again. 'Hadn't you better find out? The court of appeal started over thirty minutes ago! Please ring his home and kindly inform him that they want him there, and that he's holding things up!'

'Yes, sir.'

'And while you're about it,' Hughes added, 'ask him to phone me before he decides to grace the court with his presence!' He rang off.

'Phew,' sighed Bailey after he hung up, his youthful face sweating. He picked up the receiver again and told the operator, 'Please give me Utuka double six.' He drummed his fingers nervously on the polished surface of Mason's desk as he waited for the operator to connect him. When a few minutes passed and nothing happened, he demanded of the operator, 'Miss Ekwendu, have you rung the number I gave you?'

'Yes, Mr Bailey, but there was no reply.'

'Keep ringing it until someone answers.' He darted from Mason's office into his small adjoining one to take a confidential file from an office messenger, and then he turned to the phone.

'Mr Bailey,' the slim, attractive and newly employed Katherine Ekwendu told him, 'there's still no reply, sir, but I have to cut you off. I've other calls to put through.'

'All right, but try again after you've placed the calls.' He hung up and wondered, out loud to himself, the reason for the delay of his immediate senior officer, for Mason was noted for his punctuality. Or had Mason, Bailey thought confusedly, accompanied John MacIntosh all the way to the coast instead of to the train at Omozi? He sighed and wiped his face.

Their colleague, John MacIntosh, the lanky and zealous Assistant District Officer in charge of the affairs of the sub-station at Ukana, had been taken ill, and hurriedly sent home to Britain only the previous Saturday. MacIntosh's illness came suddenly after he and Mason had a confrontation with the tall and impressive-looking chief Obieze III. He was a local chief whose primary aims was to uphold the cultural heritage of the town over which he was the head, and who deeply resented the intrusion of foreign administrators who had arrived with their own laws. Mason, as the District Officer of the region, was on one of his frequent trips to the sub-station in which Obieze held sway.

Obieze's father, chief Obieze II, had died, and the custom required that many heads should go with the deceased chief to the grave. Trouble started when the young brother of the last man whose head was taken for the burial rites, saw and reported the matter to the Assistant District Officer, John MacIntosh, who in turn informed his visiting, immediate senior officer, Mason. From then on, the assassins, Okafor, a small, wizened but powerful town elder, and his tall commanding-looking colleague, Chukwuka, felt themselves miserable and hounded, until, with the advice of the council of elders, they took refuge in their fortresses. For it was Chukwuka who had cast a spell of juju on MacIntosh, which made the latter ill, and resulted in his being sent home to Britain. The chief himself had come in for a severe rap during the confrontation. However, the much experienced, tougher and feared Mason had smelt a rat. After seeing MacIntosh off, and unknown to his colleagues at the region's headquarters, he had quietly returned to Ukana in the early hours of the morning to investigate. It was then that he met his death – having walked into a trap, carefully set by chief Obieze and the town elders, who felt that Mason knew too much.

Bailey reached for the phone again and dialled the operator. 'Miss Ekwendu, have you had a reply yet from the District Officer's home?'

'No, not yet.'

'All right. Please connect me to the D.C.'s office.'

Seconds later the operator informed Bailey, 'I'm ringing the D.C.'s office for you now.'

'Jack Bailey here, sir,' he said as Hughes came on the line.

7

'But I thought I told you to ask Maurice to ring me?' Hughes demanded, brushing back his hair.

'Yes, sir, but he hasn't come in yet.'

'What?' Hughes asked angrily. He had untidy hair flecked with grey which he pushed perpetually away from his forehead.

Bailey was saying again, 'The operator rang his home for over five minutes, but there was no reply.'

'Has he gone on trek again?' Hughes asked.

'I don't know. I shouldn't think so. He arrived back only last Friday as you know, sir. He normally doesn't leave again without spending at least a week or two in the office.' As he looked up from the phone, and without covering the mouth of the receiver he said, 'Yes?'

'What was that?' Hughes demanded, frowning.

Bailey recollected himself and stammered, 'I'm sorry, sir. It's a reporter from *The Daily Observer*.'

'What does he want?'

'I don't exactly know. I'll find out.' Bailey looked inquiringly at the young reporter and reported back to Hughes. 'He says he's looking for news generally. He's just come down from Ukana to check up on the accuracy of the incident there.'

'What incident?'

'Hold on, sir, while I ask him.'

After a few minutes Bailey informed Hughes, 'He says he's following the news angle about MacIntosh's and Maurice's confrontation with the chief last Friday . . .'

Hughes cut in quickly, 'Did you tell him more than he knows?'

'No, sir.'

'Good. Don't. Look, put a call through to Ukana and to the other sub-stations to see whether Maurice is there. In the meantime, send a messenger to the court of appeal to tell them to go ahead with the proceedings.'

'Yes, sir.'

'And Bailey, if Maurice should come in the meantime, ask him to phone me.'

'Yes, sir.'

Hughes turned to the government surveyor, Arthur Johnson, who'd been sitting patiently waiting to have a word with him. 'Maurice is nowhere to be found.'

'He's probably sleeping off the after effects of seeing MacIntosh to the train yesterday, at the home of his lady friend,' Johnson remarked lightly and jovially without thinking, and immediately regretted his words. He tried to brush the whole thing off as inconsequential, realising in whose presence he sat. But it was too late.

Hughes stared at him with the look he always assumed when he wanted to be imperial. 'What, Maurice keep a woman?'

Johnson hesitated and shifted uncomfortably in his chair. He wished now that he hadn't made the joke, as he well knew that jokes of that sort, or of any kind at all, never went down well with Hughes. But having put his foot in it, he felt he had to go on. And from the way Hughes was looking at him, there was no escaping the man! 'From what I've heard, yes. But I wouldn't like to be quoted, George, or for it to be taken seriously,' he said uneasily, and wondered sadly what he'd started. Damn-it,' he thought hysterically, 'every man wants a woman, his wife, somebody else's or an unattached one! What difference does it make between the sheets in the long run!'

'Where does she live?' Hughes asked, grimly ignoring the ringing of his phone and the distaste the pursuit of the subject aroused in the surveyor.

'That I don't know!' Johnson almost shouted. But he got control of himself and said in a normal voice, 'If it's true, and it's a strong if, I doubt anyone knows but him. He covers his tracks pretty well. Look, George . . .'

'By that you mean he changes his women every so often?' persisted Hughes, with a look of wonder.

Johnson shifted again in his chair and fished out a cigarette. 'I don't know, George. I'm sure I'm wrong about the whole thing. One often hears a lot of things in the Club that aren't at all true.'

'I wouldn't know. I don't go near the place except to mark Empire Day and that sort of thing,' remarked Hughes in a 'holier than thou' voice.

Johnson squirmed at this thrust, but before he could reply, Mark Jenkins, the Director of Information, a tall, dark, north-country man, knocked and entered. Hughes immediately turned his attention to him. Johnson took the opportunity to escape, leaving what he came to inquire of the District Commissioner for a more propitious moment. From the way Hughes nodded absentmindedly to his 'I'll come back later', Johnson knew that Hughes had no further use for him on this particular matter, or had probably even forgotten about him.

'Mark, Maurice is nowhere to be found,' Hughes said with rage.

Jenkins blinked. 'So I've heard.'

Hughes' phone started ringing again. This time he picked up the receiver. 'Yes?'

'It's Bailey, sir. I've passed on your instruction to the law court and I've just returned from Maurice's home. The door is locked – so is the door of the servant's home.'

Hughes savoured this information for a moment and then instructed the junior secretary, 'Tell that girl on the switchboard to have all Maurice's calls redirected to me.' When he replaced the receiver he said to Jenkins, 'They seem to have both packed up and moved in with the woman!'

Jenkins looked embarrassed and averted his eyes and, with a trace of laughter in his voice said, 'I very much doubt it.'

Hughes immediately seized on Jenkins' general mien and his lack of surprise at some aspects of Mason's private life, however unproved.

'So you know he keeps a woman?' When Jenkins made no reply, Hughes said, 'God, nobody tells me anything!'

Jenkins said with reluctance, 'I did hear that he'd a lady friend at Winneba Close, but that was about four or five years back, and before my time. I doubt whether he still keeps her, and I very much doubt the authenticity of the whole story.'

'It's very odd, Mark,' said Hughes scratching his head.

'By the way, four of our court messengers are missing, as well as Nathan, our number one driver,' Jenkins broke into Hughes's thoughts to inform him.

'What? Then there's more to it than just an amorous adventure.'

'I should think so. One doesn't visit a lady friend, and I'm only repeating you, George,' said Jenkins with emphasis, 'with an entourage.'

'D'you think they went on some errand and then got stranded somewhere?' Hughes asked hopefully.

'I just don't know. Nathan always makes sure that all our vehicles are in tip-top shape.'

'Yes, he's rather good,' Hughes admitted. 'Still the unexpected does happen occasionally.'

'I agree. I think we should give the whole matter a bit more time to develop and see what happens,' suggested Jenkins.

'Right. Look, Mark, check with Jack Bailey to see whether any information has come in from the sub-stations.'

'I'll do that.'

'And send Arthur right back in here. I haven't finished with him. Fancy his leaving without telling me what he wanted.'

'Yes, George,' replied Jenkins, and inwardly said 'Hail Caesar!'

As Jenkins reached the door Hughes stopped him with, 'Look, there's a reporter from the *Observer* in the building. I don't want a whisper of this to reach his ears. I've told Jack Bailey to say nothing to the man. But I want you to make doubly certain that this is carried out.'

'Yes, George.'

The phone started ringing as Jenkins was leaving Hughes's office, and was about to shut the door behind him. Hughes called him back and motioned him to wait. Jenkins went back into the office and stood waiting in the middle of the room as Hughes spoke on the phone.

'I've now heard from the sub-stations,' began Bailey.

'Yes, yes, what did they say?'

'That they neither saw nor heard from Maurice, sir, but the message from Ukana's a bit different.'

'Well, go on, tell me what it is.'

'They saw MacIntosh and Maurice in court last Friday morning.'

'I could have told you that! You should have been aware of that too!' shouted Hughes abruptly.

'Excuse me, sir,' Bailey went on, wide-eyed with youthful innocence. 'In view of the negative replies to our inquiries from the sub-stations, d'you think it'd be to our advantage if we gave the reporter a tip-off? It might help us to find Maurice.'

Hughes, who had been listening to Bailey in stunned

11

silence, finally found his voice. 'For heaven's sake don't! Are you out of your mind? The last thing we want is to have the story plastered all over their front page. Get rid of him. Give him the government's handout on palm produce!'"

'He's left the office, sir, but he's still about the grounds.'

'Do as I say!' foamed Hughes, and slammed down the receiver. He turned to Jenkins. 'The nitwit! Have the whole matter taken out of his hands, and make sure that none of the other officials breathe a word about Maurice to him.'

'Do you mean to Bailey?' asked Jenkins.

'No, to the reporter. And to Bailey if you must,' replied Hughes, tugging at his moustache.

'It'd look odd and make the reporter suspicious if we suddenly became unfriendly. He's used to hanging around here, and has been useful to me on several occasions,' pointed out Jenkins.

'That may be so. All the same, don't let him in on this one,' Hughes said, rummaging through the papers on his desk. He looked up to inquire from Jenkins, 'Have you seen today's paper? I don't seem to have mine.'

'I gather their printing machine broke down and that the paper will be out this afternoon.'

'That's something to cheer all of us up,' said Hughes, pausing from his task. 'Do they still have the same machine that walks out of the building when the paper is being printed?'

When Jenkins answered in the affirmative, Hughes cried, 'God. Whatever shall we do with Martha-Maria?'

In their pleasant plight of trying to locate Mason, Jenkins tried not to laugh at the District Commissioner's favourite expression when exasperated.

'Shall I go now?' he asked.

'No, Mark, I want you to motor up to Ukana. The place must be in turmoil with neither MacIntosh nor Maurice there.'

'Right away.'

'Generally lock things up where necessary.'

'I'll do that.'

'Good. If the interpreter or anyone else should ask your reason for doing so, tell them it's only temporary – that we want to have the building painted. It's a flimsy excuse with the heavy rains coming soon. They will wash the blooming thing off in no time. But there it is. Not used to lying, I can't think of a more convincing explanation.' He nodded to Jenkins. 'You may go,' he added.

'Yes, George.'

'Oh, one more thing. Send out some drivers with the remaining vans on the road to the other sub-stations to see whether Maurice had a breakdown and needs towing in.'

Jenkins then left Hughes's office before the man could think up any further errands for him.

Chapter Two

Gabriel Anako, for fifteen years the court interpreter at the sub-station in Ukana, ambled his way from his small bungalow in the grounds of the native court. He stopped and looked askance at the milling crowd shouting at the top of their voices at the old night-watchman, Frederick Eze. Anako, with his balding forehead shining in the sunlight, hurried quickly to the spot to rescue the old man.

'What be reason for this?' he inquired of the crowd, after he had extricated Eze. When no answer was forthcoming, he turned to Eze. 'What happen?'

'I no know,' replied the old night-watchman, glad to be alive.

'What they say you do them?' Anako further asked.

'Nothin', ekcep' I tell them say they no go fit enter the building because the place lock.'

'Who lock him?'

'I no know who lock him. I come this morning-time and see him lock.'

The court interpreter pushed his way through the crowd and tried the door knob. When it proved to be as Eze had told him, he swung to inquire, 'But Mr MacIntosh give you key for open and sweep the court for every morning-time?'

'I know, but when I go for the small shed where I keep broom and hang key for night-time, the thin' no be there,' Eze explained.

'For which place the key go? You think somebody thief it?' Anako asked him.

'Maybe.'

'Who?'

'I no know.'

'You see anybody? Anybody at all who no look right come through the gate?'

'I no certain. Too many people come through the gate for night-time, for afternoon-time, and for morning-time.'

The court interpreter looked at his watch. 'It say half nine,' he mumbled.

The night-watchman grunted his disapproval. 'Mr Mac-Intosh for be here for nine o'clock.'

Anako faced the crowd. 'I want everybody who no get business here to go. But if you get business with native court, make you sit for under mango tree for wait. The court late small. Mr McIntosh go come soon for open door.'

There were murmurs of discontent.

'All right,' Anako told them again. 'If you think say you no go fit wait, make you go home. But when court open, it no go wait for you!' he warned.

Those that had genuine reason to be present in court that morning shuffled their way and sat under the mango tree. Others who had merely come for the day's outing, looked restlessly about them with anger and despair. They shouted, broke branches off the trees, and wondered what on earth to do with themselves for the rest of the day.

Anako turned to Eze once more. 'I no understand all this. Mr MacIntosh never come late like this before.' He thought for a while. 'I think, Eze, I go for him house for see what happen.'

He returned fifteen minutes later.

'Well?' Eze asked him.

'Nobody be for the place.'

'I surprise,' said Eze, trying desperately to find the reason for MacIntosh's lateness. 'You think maybe he go for trek?'

'If he go, he bin for tell me,' Anako informed him. 'Besides, he no go for trek when court sit.'

'So, what we do now?' asked the night-watchman, deeply worried.

Anako spread his hands. 'I no know, but we wait for inside shed.'

When they got inside the night-watchman's shed Eze began to roll tobacco. As he did so a thought came to him in a flash. When he could contain it no longer, he turned to Anako and come out with it. 'I no think say, I go fit swear to it just now, Mr Anako, but I think I hear van make noise for night-time yesterday.'

Anako looked at him sharply. 'For which place you hear noise?'

'That be the thing,' said Eze, as he spat out bits of tobacco. 'I no know if it be for main road or for inside native court ground I hear noise. But I think it be for native court here.'

'You no check for see,' Anako asked. Eze shook his head and went on to enlighten the court interpreter further. 'But I no think say, the driver take the van come out for night-time yesterday. I see him this morning-time when he give engine water, and I ask him if he want for go any place. He tell me no. He just give engine water. I no think say he go any place for two week."

They sat in silence for a time. Anako suddenly looked up and pricked up his ears, his senses alert. 'I think I hear phone ring.'

'Eh?' asked Eze, who was about to set a match to his rolled-up tobacco.

'Shssh,' said Anako, waving for silence. 'I think the phone for Mr MacIntosh him office ring.'

'How we go fit enter the place for answer phone?'

The court interpreter thought for a second and then recalled that the fanlight in MacIntosh's office was always left open. The man had a thing about stuffiness. Anako turned to Eze and instructed him, 'Make you go bring driver come. He young, and him body go fit go through fanlight.'

Eze shuffled away and returned with Christopher Odu, the sub-station's only driver.

'The phone for Mr MacIntosh office ring, and we want hear what phone say,' Anako informed him.

'You no get key?' Odu asked, a little annoyed.

'No,' Anako replied and went on to explain, 'We no get time for waste. Mr MacIntosh no come for court yet, and him phone ring.'

They all listened for a while. 'You hear, he still ring,' Anako added and turned to Eze. 'For which place you keep ladder?'

'That be him for behin' you,' said Eze pointing.

Anako swung round and looked at it. 'O.K. Make you carry him,' he ordered the night-watchman. They then left for MacIntosh's office. The ladder was set up and Odu climbed up, eased his lean body through the open fanlight and jumped down. Once in he spread his hands to say that he didn't know what to do next. Anako tapped on the glass window and signalled him to open it. Odu nodded comprehendingly and a smile of relief spread over his face.

Anako got in through the now open window and picked up the receiver. 'Ukana ten!' he shouted.

'Is that Ukana?' asked the telephone operator at Utuka.

'Yes, yes ; this be Ukana ten. What say?'

'Please hold the line.'

'O.K.'

Another voice came on the line. 'This is Bailey from the region's headquarters.'

To Eze and the driver Anako whispered in an aside, 'Bailey, I no know the man.' He riveted his attention on the phone. 'What say?'

'I said is the District Officer there?'

'Mr Mason?' Anako asked.

'Yes,' Bailey replied.

'No, sir, he no be here. And Mr MacIntosh no be here also.'

'Yes, I know that, but I want to know whether Mr Mason is.'

'That, I no fit say. He no come in with Mr MacIntosh yet.'

'Yes, I know that Mr MacIntosh isn't there. We don't expect him to be there. All I want to know is whether Mr Mason is.'

'You want make I call Mr Mason, sir?'

'Is he there then?'

'No, sir, he no come in with Mr MacIntosh yet.'

'Blimey,' muttered Bailey as he loosened his tie. 'Look,' he continued, 'what I want to know is whether you've seen Mr Mason there this morning.'

'Mr Mason come for court with Mr MacIntosh.'

'He's there then?'

'No, sir.'

'When d'you expect him to arrive?'

'For this morning-time.'

'But he hasn't?'

'No, sir.'

'I see,' said Bailey. He continued after a pause. 'Look, send someone to see whether he's still at the residence of the Assistant District Officer.'

'I send somebody.'

'Yes, and I'll hold on until the person returns.'

'But I send somebody.'

'Yes, you've told me that!' Bailey shouted angrily.

'I go for residence and come back,' Anako informed him quietly.

'Oh I see. You've already been to the residence but Mr Mason wasn't there.'

'Yes, sir.'

'You mean he's there?'

'No, sir. And the door lock. And him cook door lock also.'

'To whom am I speaking?'

'Anako here.'

'Who?'

'Interpreter for court.'

'Oh I see. So you say that you've seen nothing of the District Officer?'

'And Mr A.D.O.,' Anako thought it his duty to add.

'I see. Look, should Mr Mason arrive, will you please ask him to phone Utuka.'

'Mr Mason come for court last Friday.'

'Yes I know that. He has since returned to headquarters.'

'What say?'

'Never mind, just ask him to ring me when he turns up in court.'

'Yes, sir.'

'Right.'

Anako, having climbed out of MacIntosh's office via the same window through which he had entered, murmured with a superior air, 'Bailey, Bailey,' and gazed upwards with his head thrown back. 'Mr MacIntosh no tell me anything about Mr Bailey before!' he said to his listeners, Eze and Odu, who were farther down than he on the rungs of the job ladder.

'What he say him want?' Odu, the driver, asked.

'Bailey?' Anako asked back with a touch of familiarity in his voice, as he spoke the junior secretary's surname. When his audience nodded, and looked on expectantly, the court interpreter went on. 'The District Officer,' he replied, clearly aware that Eze, the night-watchman, and Odu, the driver, were watching him with awe at the thought of his having conducted a conversation with headquarters. In all probability, and for all the often secretive interpreter cared to tell them, he may have even held the conversation with the D.C. himself.

When minutes passed in which the other two thought that Anako was holding something vital back from them, the night-watchman could stand the suspense no longer, and so he asked, 'What you tell him?'

That seemed to recall Anako from where he got to. 'Eh, oh, Bailey! I tell him say D.O. no be for here. *I* think they look for D.O.'

'And what him say? The Bailey man I mean?' the inquisitive Eze went on. But before the court interpreter could reply, Odu, the driver, asked. 'You tell Mr Bailey say court lock?'

Anako slapped his forehead. 'Ah! I forget!' he shouted.

'You see what I see?' Eze whispered.

'Eh? For which place?' Anako asked quickly.

'New white man just come out from him motor car,' Eze said, pointing. They all stood stock still and watched as Jenkins tried the doorknob of the main entrance to the native court. As he did so, Anako came out of his trance and found his feet. He went forward and the two others followed.

'Excuse me, sir,' Anako began, 'you want something?'

'Who are you?' Jenkins turned and asked. He had barely finished speaking when he realised that he was addressing a fellow government employee, for Anako's khaki ensemble with the crown emblazoned in red on the left breast pocket made that obvious.

'I be interpreter for court,' Anako said with barely concealed anger in his voice, annoyed that who he was was not immediately recognised by the stranger.

Jenkins winced at this. 'I see,' he said. 'Have you seen the District Officer?' he asked.

'No, sir, but I just finish talk now-now to Mr Bailey for Utuka.'

'Ah, Bailey has been in touch with you.'

'Yes, sir.'

'You haven't seen Mr Mason?' Jenkins asked again.

'I see him last Friday.'

'Not since then?'

'No, sir.'

Jenkins rubbed his chin thoughtfully and looked about him. 'Are all those people sitting under the tree waiting for court to start?'

'Yes, sir. I tell them for wait.'

'Better tell them that all the cases are suspended until further notice and to go home.'

When Anako looked at Jenkins wonderingly, Jenkins saw that further explanations were required of him. 'We want to have the building painted.'

'Governor go come?' Anako asked.

This question threw Jenkins momentarily off balance. He was torn between saying yes, thereby giving more weight to the reason for painting the court. He soon recovered himself and replied. 'Not for a while yet, certainly not this year,' he said nervously, aware that three pairs of eyes were watching like hawks.

'But rain go soon come,' Anako pointed out, and went on to explain, 'It not wise for paint building just before rain come. Paint building all right for dry season, not rainy season.'

Jenkins swallowed, and wondered what he'd walked into.

'Yes I realise that,' he agreed. 'All the same the D.C. wants just one coat of paint on all the sub-station law courts,' he said, and flushed.

The worried crease eased from Anako's face. 'Ah,' he said, swallowing the lie.

'Yes,' Jenkins replied, looking foolish but relieved. 'I see the main door to the court is locked. Anyway, I've come to lock up any other place that's lockable,' he told Anako as he took a step forward.

The night-watchman jumped in to ask Jenkins, 'But how we go paint the building if you lock the place? All the place lock already, and the key no be for here.'

'Oh?' Jenkins said. It was all he could think of saying.

'Yes, sir,' Eze went on in his rasping voice. 'Mr Anako climb window for answer Mr MacIntosh him phone.'

'Where's the keys then?'

'I no know, sir. I no seen them this morning when I went for open court.'

'Where d'you normally keep him?' Jenkins asked, shocked at the news of the lost keys.

'For shed. The same place I keep broom and sit for watch for night-time.'

'You think someone may've taken them?'

'Yes, sir,' Eze replied, hoping this would clear him from being accused of negligence. So relieved was he at this probability that Jenkins' next question caught him by surprise.

'Who?'

'I no know,' he replied with an innocent look after he recovered.

'Why not?' Jenkins asked, bearing down on him angrily. 'You're the night-watchman as well as the janitor, going by the records. So you should be able to tell me how and when the keys disappeared.'

'You see, sir,' Eze went on by way of explanation, 'I not young man. I not fit open my eye all the time for night-time.'

'You think someone may've taken the keys while you were having a nap?'

Relief made Eze weak. 'Yes, sir!'

Jenkins pulled him up sharply with his next chastisement. 'Negligence in a government employee is a serious offence, you know?' And promptly felt silly at having to say this to an old night-watchman, who in all probability didn't understand what he was talking about. On the night-watchman the chastisement was equally wasted, like water off a duck's back, as Jenkins thought, for he asked, 'What say, sir?'

Jenkins looked away from Eze and didn't reply. He found the whole thing a bit incongruous, with a certain amount of inexplicable crudity. 'You're Mr Anako?' he turned to ask the court interpreter. Anako nodded, and looked pleased. 'Who d'you think could have taken the keys?'

Anako let out his breath. 'I no know, sir.'

'D'you often get prowlers here?'

'Ah, no, sir, they 'fraid.'

'Wait master,' Eze broke in. 'I think I remember some-thin'. I tell Mr Anako for this morning-time say, I hear van noise. But I no certain if van make noise for main road or for inside here.'

Jenkins' interest rose immediately. 'Oh? You heard a van start up?'

'Yes, sir. I not certain when I tell Mr Anako before. But now, I certain.'

Jenkins thought for a while. 'But you told me only a little while back that you neither heard nor saw anyone remove the keys from the shed. If you didn't hear that, and with you sitting beside the keys in the shed, how could you have possibly heard the noise made by the van?'

Eze moved his head from side to side impatiently. 'That be so, sir. But I certain now I hear van noise.'

Jenkins sighed. 'What did you do when you heard the noise?'

'I no do nothin',' Eze replied unruffled.

'But surely it's your responsibility to check the slightest noise day or night on the grounds of the law court?'

Eze was saved from replying by Anako's interruption. 'I see man who come all the time for ask question about court.' Jenkins followed the court interpreter's eyes.

It was Godfrey Onyeso, the reporter Hughes had asked Jenkins to get rid of from the government offices at Utuka. As the tall and lithe Onyeso walked up, Jenkins told Anako to go and tell the people waiting in the shade, to go home. To Eze and Odu, he said that they should go about their business. As a parting shot he warned the three, 'I don't want what we discussed just now to reach the ears of the man approaching!'

The three nodded and left.

Jenkins was smiling as Onyeso reached him. 'We meet again, Godfrey,' he said with the ease he didn't feel.

Onyeso returned his smile. 'Yes.'

'Were you by any chance following me?' Jenkins asked blandly.

Onyeso eyed him. 'How d'you mean?'

'Come clean,' said Jenkins with a set chin.

Onyeso allowed himself a little smile as he replied, 'You seem to forget that I'm the region's chief reporter for my paper.'

'I don't dispute that,' replied Jenkins dryly. The tone of Jenkin's voice was not lost on Onyeso, for the reporter replied, 'Well, if you must know, and if it'll help you to sleep better, I've merely come to check on the validity of the story that Chief Obieze was carpeted by the District Officer and his assistant last Friday,' said Onyeso with a grin.

Jenkins was immediately put out. 'Who told you?' he asked before he could stop himself.

Onyeso stared steadily at the face of the Director of Information. 'I've my methods,' he said at last.

'That I don't doubt,' Jenkins replied, somewhat recovered. 'It was nothing much ; purely a misunderstanding on both sides,' he added as he felt that he must say something, however evasive, for he'd known the reporter a long time.

'Sure?' asked Onyeso sceptically.

Jenkins looked rattled. 'Of course I'm sure. D'you doubt me?'

'That wasn't what I heard,' Onyeso said calmly, enjoying himself.

Jenkins raised his brows and brushed back his hair. 'Oh? What did you hear?'

'Mine's to obtain information, not to give it.'

Jenkins suppressed a smile. 'Take it from me, Godfrey, the mishap wasn't much.'

'Surely you can trust me,' Onyeso countered.

'Several heads, as you well know, went with the late Chief to his grave, and that was all it was about.'

'I see,' replied Onyeso, looking about him. 'Isn't the court sitting today? Why is everyone leaving?'

'No, the court isn't sitting today. We've got to paint the building.'

'I see,' Onyeso murmured.

Thank heaven for that! thought Jenkins privately. He excused himself and escaped before the full force of his weightless excuse struck Onyeso full in the face.

As he left Onyeso he saw Anako, the only responsible government employee now in Ukana, approaching. Jenkins took him out of sight and hearing to have a final word with him.

Onyeso stood and watched, and as he watched his suspicion grew deeper, and the excuse Jenkins had given him for sending everyone home became even more flimsy.

Chapter Three

Obieze, having finished his breakfast, and with nothing urgently requiring his attention, decided to call in and see one of his wives who had been shunning his advances lately.

Of all his eight wives, this one presented him with the greatest trouble. Either she must submit, or leave his compound. After all, he wasn't her brother, but her husband.

This problem so dominated his mind as he circled his vast compound on his way to this particular wife's house, that he started when out of nowhere, and so unexpectedly, a panting runner stood before him.

'Eh?' the Chief demanded.

'Chief, they close native court,' the man said breathlessly.

The harsh words Obieze was about to pour on the man for having interrupted his journey and intruded on his thoughts, died instantly in his throat. 'Who close court?'

The informer took a deep breath to steady himself before he replied. 'I no know – nobody know. Interpreter tell all the people way get business for court, make them go home.'

Obieze paused to digest this information fully. 'You mean we no get court here anymore?' he asked in surprise, his thoughts scattered.

The informer had now gained proper control of himself, so he replied in a normal voice, 'Me no know that. All I hear I tell you. I hear say they want for paint the place.'

'Paint!' shouted Obieze in disbelief. 'But the place no dirty!' Then the thought came to him that with MacIntosh gone, and Mason, unknown to his colleagues, out of the way, the region's headquarters would use painting the building as an excuse until a new man was appointed to replace MacIntosh and Mason. The anxiety Obieze felt at the outset left him. He was completely relaxed now. He afforded himself the luxury of a smile at a job well executed as far as his helping to get rid of MacIntosh, doing away with Mason, and putting the headquarters in complete disarray was concerned.

The informer, obeying the unwritten law that no one must interrupt a chief or speak without first being spoken to by His Highness, stood waiting Obieze's pleasure. But when something that seemed to him like eternity had passed, and since the next bit of information he was itching to give Obieze was very vital, he coughed discreetly to make the ruler aware that he was still standing there, and also to save himself from breaking the law. This diplomacy brought instant result. For Obieze murmured, 'They lie, Foreigner lie too much!'

After this the informer felt he could now impart to the Chief the vital information he could no longer contain, and which was about to strangle him.

'Chief Obieze, I think I also for tell you say, another white man come for court this morning-time, and I think he still be there.'

'Eh?' responded Obieze with shock.

Encouraged by this reaction the informer went on. 'He be still there when I lef for come here.'

'What the man look like?' Obieze asked, his shock deepening.

The informer scratched his head in an attempt to recall any outstanding feature of the visiting expatriate. Finally he voiced what he could recall. 'All white man look like the same to me,' he began, 'but this one long, and he get black-hair.'

Obieze frowned and looked as if he was trying to put a name to the expatriate's face, or to remember whether he'd come across Jenkins before. When neither prospect proved successful he said, 'I no think say I see this new man before. You think he be new A.D.O.?'

To this his informer replied, 'Ah, that I no fit say. I no wait for hear.'

'What be him name?'

'That too I no wait for hear.'

'I want make you go back find out for me.'

'Yes, Chief.'

As his informer began to retreat, Obieze charged him with further responsibility. 'Wait!' he ordered. 'Make you

24

tell Anako, but make you no tell him in front of new white man, you hear?' he warned, and the informer nodded. 'I want make you tell Anako say I want him for come to see me for afternoon time today.'

The informer left for the native court.

'You understand my instructions?' Jenkins once more asked the court interpreter.

'Yes, sir.'

'Good. You're not to tell anyone anything about the missing keys until we know ourselves at headquarters.' When Anako said he understood, Jenkins continued. 'By the way, Mr MacIntosh is on leave . . .'

Anako cut it with, 'Leave? But Mr MacIntosh just come. He no be for here long to go leave!'

Jenkins was momentarily silenced, and then tried to explain as best he could, averting his eyes from those of the court interpreter. 'I know, Mr Anako, but these things happen.'

'He go come back, from the leave I mean?'

'Er . . . I don't really know. We'll have to wait and see.'

Anako was no fool. He'd heard the hesitancy in Jenkins' voice, and caught the point from his fifteen years of experience of seeing A.D.O.'s come and go.

'Maybe we go get another A.D.O.?' he pursued sadly.

Jenkins thought 'what the hell!' Why not tell the poor man the truth. After all, he's worked for the regional government for long enough. 'Yes, I think so, Mr Anako,' he replied.

This statement from Jenkins saddened Anako deeply. 'Ah, Mr MacIntosh, he be good man,' he said regretfully.

'Undoubtedly.'

'What say?'

'Yes, Mr Anako, Mr MacIntosh is a very nice man indeed.'

'Maybe you go come here yourself for replacement?' Anako asked Jenkins, looking up hopefully at him to confirm it.

'I doubt it. My line's entirely different. Look, I must get back to Utuka. The headquarters will be in touch with you.'

'How for do about Mr MacIntosh him office?'

'Oh yes. Let me have a look at it.'

'But it lock,' Anako reminded him.

'Yes. I'm aware of that. I just want to have a look at it from the outside.'

As he and the interpreter walked, Jenkins turned to him and asked, 'By the way, is the window through which you got in still open?'

Anako confirmed this. 'Fanlight open too,' he told Jenkins. When they reached the open window Anako climbed in after Jenkins. They looked round and found everything in order.

'Look, we'll have to close the fanlight and just leave the window half open so you can get in should you receive a call from headquarters.'

'All right, sir.'

Jenkins gathered what confidential papers he could find and prepared to leave. He had his feet on the window ledge ready to jump down when Onyeso mysteriously appeared. They stared at each other. Onyeso burst out laughing. 'A government employee burgling government premises! That should make a good headline and interesting reading! I wish I'd a photographer with me to put it on celluloid!'

Jenkins looked embarrassed. 'Look, Godfrey . . .' he began, but didn't know how to continue.

'Isn't it odd,' Onyeso went on, pressing his advantage, 'that a law court still in session, at least it was sitting up to last Friday, should be locked suddenly in order to have it painted?'

'Odd indeed, but odder things have happened. Godfrey, these things do happen,' replied Jenkins when he had recovered himself and jumped down from the window ledge.

'What things?' Onyeso persisted.

'My friend you ask too many questions!' Anako piped up from behind Jenkins.

'It's quite all right, Mr Anako. I'll take care of this,' Jenkins told him. As he straightened up he continued, 'It so happens that most of these cases here should really now go to the court of appeal at Utuka. All that's left here at the moment are merely petty thefts and things like that.'

'But you have no keys?' Onyeso asked with feigned innocence. 'You've just jumped out through an office window,' he pointed out to Jenkins as if to refresh the latter's memory.

'You're absolutely right,' Jenkins replied with equilibrium

and went on. 'And that's my privilege. But if you must know, I forgot the keys at Utuka in my hurry. It's just one of those things.'

'But surely the resident official . . .' Onyeso started, and Jenkins finished it for him. 'He's on leave,' replied Jenkins. 'He left the keys quite rightly with headquarters before he departed.'

'But the relief and the official stationed here are always together for a short period for the handing over,' Onyeso stubbornly pressed on.

Jenkins wiped perspiration from his eyes as he answered. 'Yes. Mr MacIntosh however had to take his leave quickly, while there's a lull.' He suddenly became angry. 'Look here, Godfrey. I've told you the truth and all I know. You can either take it or leave it.'

'Well, I'll leave you to it,' replied the reporter, and walked off.

'Foolish man!' said Anako.

'Let's leave the matter there, Mr Anako,' said Jenkins as he saw the anger in the interpreter's face. 'Oh he'll make trouble for us. Well,' continued Jenkins, looking about him. 'I leave the premises in your hands. We'll be in touch with you from headquarters as soon as possible.'

'All right, sir.'

Onyeso, having left Jenkins and Anako, ambled his way around the court grounds. His sharpened mind did not for one minute believe what Jenkins had told him. The more he thought about it, the more fishy it became, so he determined to find out the truth.

'You're the night-watchman?' Onyeso asked, as he came upon old Eze. 'Yes, and janitor. What you want?' Eze wanted to know.

'I want you to do me a favour.'

'Who me?' asked Eze, aghast.

'Yes you,' Onyeso told him, slightly amused at the startled look on the old man's face.

'Well, what dash [bribe] you want?' Eze asked, frowning, and Onyeso realised that the man had misunderstood his words. He burst out laughing as the full meaning of the situation hit him.

'I didn't mean that I wanted you to give me a dash. I'm the one who'll give you the dash if you do me a . . .' he stopped as he searched for a simpler word which the night-watchman would understand. 'A small favour,' he finished patiently.

The alarmed expression on Eze's face at the thought of giving anyone dash out of his seven and sixpence monthly wage, relaxed, and he replied in a more friendly voice, 'Ah, now I follow you!'

'Good.' Onyeso then went on to enlighten him, 'I want you to tell me the real reason behind the court being painted.'

'Ah, Mr . . .'

'Onyeso.'

'Mr Onyeso, I no fit tell you,' said Eze without thinking.

Onyeso's mouth twitched. His eyes danced viciously as he cornered Eze further. 'Why can't you tell me?'

'The white man way jus' lef say make we no say any-thing to anybody if anybody ask,' Eze continued stupidly.

'So there's another reason then?'

'Yes, I mean No!' Eze shouted on realising his indis-cretion, and threw away his tooth pick. But Onyeso, hav-ing trapped his man, pressed on, this time with the added temptation of a cash reward thrown in. 'I'll give you one pound a month as a retainer fee if you tell me.'

Eze swivelled his eyes to look Onyeso fully in the face. Was the man mad, he thought, or was he deceiving him? When he saw neither on Onyeso's face, and also took in the immaculate, and for him, expensive robe and trousers the reporter was wearing, he asked thickly, 'One pound every month?' He'd never seen or handled such a lump sum at one go in his life. When Onyeso nodded with seriousness at the query, Eze looked at him, open mouthed. One pound just for simple information, with more to come each month! He looked mesmerised. 'Jesu cry!' he shouted at last, and rubbed his nose.

'Well?' Onyeso asked after minutes, when it seemed that Eze had completely disappeared into a dream world and had forgotten his presence.

'Mr Onyeso,' Eze began sorrowfully, 'I no fit,' he added with a shake of his head, having searched his soul.

'Why not?' Onyeso asked.

'Because Mr Jenkin way jus' lef go sack me if he find out say I tell you,' he explained with an effort. The anguish of

28

letting a pound enter and slip out of his hands was too great.

'Look, if you tell me I won't let anyone else know that it was you who gave me the information,' persuaded Onyeso. Eze looked up and searched the reporter's face. He began to think again. This new proposition certainly appealed to him. He cast his eyes on the ground to consider it further. He jerked his head up suddenly to express another vital point. 'But you go put it for paper,' he reminded Onyeso, his eyes narrowing at the corners.

'True, but I won't reveal my source of information. I won't betray you now, or in the future, ever,' he told Eze softly.

Eze inclined his head as this sank in. He straightened up and thought of the things he could do with twenty shillings a month. The more he thought, the more the temptation to accept proved too great to resist. He could quit the job here as night-watchman cum janitor for the mere pittance of seven and six a month, and his stomach swollen night after night from the cold wind. But he threw that idea right out of his mind. If he did that the man standing before him would no longer be interested in him, and would withdraw his proposition. There would be no access for him to obtain the necessary information that he was willing to pay so handsomely for.

Another line of thought came to him as he stood, deciding. He suddenly remembered that the season for planting crops was upon them and that the additional money would go a long way to help him out. He looked about him to see if Anako or the driver were watching. When he saw neither he edged closer to this new benefactor and cleared his throat. 'I go take the one pound. What you want for know?'

Onyeso, who had watched the struggle taking place in the night-watchman, and also witnessed the devil successfully gaining the upper hand, now murmured, 'I've told you before. I want to know the truth about what's happening here.'

'Give me the money first,' Eze said, with a snap of his fingers.

Onyeso hedged. 'Don't you trust me?'

Eze rubbed his eyes. 'I do Mr Onyeso, I do. But that no be for here or for there. I want make we finish the money palaver side first.'

A crisp pound note changed hands. Eze glanced about him furtively as he folded the note and tucked it into his lappa. He smirked his lips with satisfaction when the task was completed. His breathing became normal again. 'Mr MacIntosh go for leave, Mr Mason they no fit find. Somebody thief key.'

'What d'you mean about the D.O.?' Onyeso asked his man. The news about Mason was unexpected, and of more interest.

'They say they no see him for headquarter,' Eze said impatiently, anxious to get away in case someone saw him talking to the newspaper man.

'Oh? When was he missed?'

'That I no know. I think they 'fraid he loss, or they no go worry so.' And with that Eze walked off to sweep up the leaves from under the trees.

Arthur Johnson, the government surveyor, knocked and entered the expansive office of the District Commissioner. Hughes watched his approach from behind his huge desk flanked on either side with leather chairs. He was a man of medium height when he stood up, but gave the impression of being tall as he sat behind his desk.

'You asked to see me?' said Johnson.

'Yes,' Hughes replied abstractedly, and added, 'Please sit down.'

'Thank you.'

The District Commissioner looked at some folders on his desk. He folded them and sat back in his seat. 'It's been suggested that the soil here might be good for rubber planting. What d'you think?'

Johnson looked at him sharply. 'You mean the soil here at Utuka?'

'No, generally.'

Johnson considered for a moment. 'I can't really say until I've tested the soil in other parts, but this area is definitely out of the question. The soil is barren. One has only to look at the harvest each year to see that.'

'Hmm,' mumbled Hughes, but Johnson added hastily. 'Idom may be different. The yams grow to nearly three feet tall there. The circumference varies of course. Still, it's a rich harvest. I've seen them at the market.'

'Is that so? I wonder why nothing grows very much here despite all the hard work the local people put in, and the heavy rainfall?' Hughes wondered.

'It's just barren, I suppose.'

'Cultivation won't help?'

'We've tried that,' Johnson told him. 'We got the yams to grow just eight inches but no more. Two inches better than is normally produced by the locals.'

'Pity,' Hughes replied, looking again at the folders on his desk. 'Going back to rubber,' he went on, closing the folders once more. 'How soon can you leave to sample the soil at the place you mentioned?'

'Idom? Now if you like.'

'That's a bit quick,' Hughes told him slightly amused as he wondered whether it was he who was driving the other man away, or if it was just enthusiasm for his job.

Johnson replied with equilibrium. 'You sounded urgent when you mentioned the project.'

'Yes I know. I get all sorts of orders and requests from the Governor. I'm sure he thinks I've nothing else to do but sit here and wait for his commands!'

Johnson forced down the laugh that came to his voice and said, 'I could leave for Idom this morning to start the necessary tests if you want me to.'

'You know the place well of course. D'you have any particular ground that you consider suitable? That is if the decision to experiment in rubber became definite.'

'There's a stretch of land a mile long of very good earth between Idom and Uru. In fact one can't go wrong in that area as far as other produce is concerned. Rubber is something different.'

'I see,' said Hughes. 'Well, I've leave it in your hands.'

'Will that be all?' Johnson asked, preparing to get up.

Hughes looked up from the folder. 'For the time being, yes.'

Johnson stood up to leave. He added as an afterthought, 'I think, George, I may as well survey the land I mentioned while I'm about it.'

'How long will that take you?'

'Oh, allowing for delays and various other things, I should say a fortnight.'

'But you've only just returned from trek last week. Why not have a week's break before you set out again.'

Johnson inwardly moaned at the idea of Hughes showing some concern on his behalf. Aloud he said, 'It doesn't matter,' and added, 'By the way, why I called earlier was to tell you that I'd some unfinished business in Ichara and wished to go back. However, it'll keep in view of the rubber venture.'

Hughes' hazel eyes looked at him uncomprehendingly for a minute. 'Oh yes, I remember now, I did tell Mark to ask you if you'd be kind enough to call back.'

That's not the way it was related to me, thought Johnson, but what does it matter? He left the Commissioner's office for his own home to prepare for the trip.

He went through the lounge and up a flight of stairs to the main bedroom. As usual, Evelyn Johnson was sunbathing on the small balcony off their bedroom, with only a towel resting carelessly between her thighs, and the magazine, *Home from Home*, lying beside her. Johnson sighed and eyed her. What if their cook or steward wandered in as servants often did unexpectedly, and saw her in that pose? he asked himself. A thought occurred to him which sent sparks of shock right through him as he stood gazing at the exquisite figure of his wife. He shook his head, as if by doing so he would shake the unpalatable thought off. No! he nearly screamed out, Evelyn couldn't descend that low— or could she? He'd heard of some wives button-holing their servants while their husbands' backs were turned ; the myth, or the reality being that men in this hemisphere went much longer than their counterparts in the west.

Mrs Johnson almost leapt as she heard her husband's voice say in controlled rage, 'I'm off to survey a field at Idom for rubber planting and you're coming with me! I want no further gossip or near scandal behind my back. Take everything you'll require. We'll be away for two weeks or more, depending.' And I'll also be out of the D.C.'s reach, he added to himself.

'That awful place?' Mrs Johnson asked after she heard her husband out. 'There'll hardly be a soul in that rest house but us, or me, for most of the time!'

Johnson looked as if he couldn't care less if she stayed alone in the rest house until doomsday. 'That awful place, as you put it my darling, also pays for our bread and butter!' he snapped.

'I know, you've told me before,' Evelyn Johnson replied, getting up.

'Good. I'm glad it's sunk in,' said Johnson sarcastically. He was determined to hurt her, and hurt her deeply.

'I'll pack a case,' she replied, trailing the towel behind her from the balcony into their bedroom.

Johnson, having finished packing his own case, went downstairs to tell their cook to be ready in ten minutes with some utensils, and whatever food they had in the larder, to accompany them on trek. To their steward he said to come up in about five minutes to pick up the cases. He went back to their bedroom to find his wife in only her panties and brassiere brushing her shoulder-length hair before the dressing-table mirror.

'I wish you'd hurry,' he told her. 'I want to reach Idom before it gets too hot.'

'All in good time,' she replied lazily, laying the brush aside and picking up her lipstick.

Johnson looked at her as if he wanted to strangle her. Instead he said, 'I told Louis to come up in five minutes to pick up our cases.'

'Well, I'm ready,' said Mrs Johnson, as she rose from the dressing table. Her husband watched as she buttoned her slim figure into a canary yellow cotton frock. In another minute Louis knocked and went in and out again with the cases.

Walking behind her to their car Johnson remarked, 'I wish you'd stop using that awful hair dye or whatever it is you use on your hair. I know you were once a redhead, but your hair's now the colour of a watered-down carrot.'

Evelyn Johnson walked straight ahead without turning her head. 'Watered-down carrot indeed! Planting vegetables has ruined your eyesight, Arthur. I'm only twenty-six and neither use, nor do I need, a hair dye,' she hissed back at him.

Mrs Johnson was years younger than her husband, a fact that had pleased him at first, but which he now resented, as every male eye in the residential area and in the catering rest houses elsewhere, always rested on her with undisguised lust. Husband and wife got in their car and drove all the way to Idom in complete silence.

Hughes picked up his receiver. 'Extension two, please.'

Jack Bailey came on the line. 'Yes, sir?'

'Is Mark back yet?'

'No, sir.'

'Have him call me when he gets back.'

'Yes, sir.'

As Bailey was about to ring off, Hughes added, 'By the way, phone Ukana again will you, and tell whoever's there to inform the Chief about the temporary closure of the court. If Mark's still there when you get through, ask him to do it – if not, anyone will do,' said Hughes and rang off.

Bailey looked at his watch. It said twelve fifteen. Another hour and forty-five minutes and I'll be off for the day, and away from Hughes, he thought to himself, and placed the call to Ukana. He looked around for something to do to make him look busy while the call went through. As he did so, two of the drivers sent out on routes that Mason could have taken to any one of the five sub-stations, excluding Ukana, returned, but with no heartening news. He decided against intruding on Hughes yet, until all the drivers were back.

Chapter Four

Anako leaned against the mango tree surveying the court premises. He had never seen it so deserted before during the day. His heart was particularly heavy at the thought of MacIntosh not coming back, and enquiries being made about Mason. He had never known headquarters to be so worried before. The look on Jenkins's face also told him that the man was worried about something.

So involved was he with his private thoughts that he nearly jumped on hearing a man clear his throat behind him. He swung round immediately and demanded, 'What you want?'

'Mr Anako, Chief Obieze say him want to see you for afternoon-time today.'

'Why you no come for my front? Why you creep from behind my back for tell me, hmm? What I do way Chief want to see me?' he asked with a frown.

'You no do nothing,' he assured the court interpreter. 'I just think Chief want to see you. I sorry, Mr Anako if I make you 'fraid,' he apologised.

Anako looked relieved, but his feeling of relief was short lived as the messenger asked in the next breath, 'Who be the man who come here for this morning?'

Anako's eyes narrowed and his breathing came fast. Was the caller asking this only for his own private knowledge? He searched his companion's face but it told him nothing. 'I no know ; I no see him before today! he say him name is Jenkin.' He had scarcely finished speaking when the phone in MacIntosh's office started to ring again. He excused himself and went to answer it. The caller watched him with set face and harsh eyes.

'Anako here,' he began.

'It's Bailey again.'

'Ah, Mr Bailey!' intoned Anako in a voice of one speaking to a long-lost friend.

'Look Mr Anako, will you please inform the Chief that the court is only closed temporarily for repairs and painting.'

'Repair?' shouted the court interpreter from his end. 'Which repair? The place no leak. Mr Jenkin only say for painting.'

'All right,' sighed Bailey, 'for painting then.'

'I see,' replied Anako thoughtfully. What is happening? he asked himself, when officials from headquarters contradict each other?

He brought his attention back to Bailey who was saying, 'Is Mr Jenkins still there with you?'

'No, he left.'

'How long ago?'

'Three quarter minute,' he replied, and added as an afterthought, 'Chief Obieze say he want for see me. He send messenger for come tell me.'

'Oh, what about?'

'I no know.'

'Don't forget that you're carrying a message to him too.'

'No, I no go forget.'

Eze met him as he finished speaking and was climbing out from the window. Anako immediately told him: 'I want for see you!'

'Eh? What you want see me for?' the night-watchman asked as he took a step backwards and licked his dry lips. His heart went cold as his mind went to the pound safely hidden in his loin cloth. He could hear the thud of his heart beating in his ears.

'I want make you sit for under Mr MacIntosh office window for hear and tell me when phone ring.' As he listened to Anako's instructions, Eze gulped, and his facial muscles relaxed. 'Eh?' he asked, shocked.

'All the time. From morning until night-time, because the window open and I no want anybody go there for thief.'

'How I go do if I want piss? You want make I jus' sit there?' the night-watchman asked in astonishment.

Anako had had enough. He swung round and faced him. 'My friend we get plenty thing for do, and you worry only about piss!' he shouted, and paused, and then went on in a lower tone: 'Chief Obieze say he want to for see me. I want go home chop first. When I see him finish, then I go begin for look for labourer for start paint native court.'

'We no get white chalk. The one way we bin get for shed finish,' Eze reminded him.

'That no matter. All the labourers go get some before they start for paint.'

'Me self hungry, Mr Anako. You think say, I fit go home for chop before I sit under window?'

Anako nodded his permission. 'Make you go home and come back quick. But make you tell the driver before you go, say, to sit under window until you come back.'

Jenkins drove furiously back to Utuka. He got there just in time, in another five minutes the offices would have closed. He took the steps two at a time. On reaching the District Commissioner's office he knocked, opened the door slightly and asked, 'May I come in, George?'

'Yes, by all means,' replied Hughes as he looked up and saw who it was.

'I passed Bailey on the stairs but didn't have time to stop.

He mentioned, however, that you asked to see me as soon as I returned, and anyway I was on my way.'

'Yes, well?'

'The premises are already locked . . .'

'Good,' Hughes interrupted. He was about to broach another matter when Jenkins began again, 'It's locked, George, but not by any of our men.'

Hughes looked at him inquiringly. 'What?'

'Just as I said, everywhere is closed and the keys are nowhere to be found.'

'They can't be,' shouted Hughes. 'How's that possible?'

Jenkins spread his hands. 'I don't know.'

Hughes snapped his fingers suddenly. 'Now wait a minute, I remember that I told Maurice to drive up to Ukana to collect MacIntosh's U.K. things and to lock up the place.'

Both men sighed and relaxed. 'That explains it,' said Jenkins. 'I must confess that I was staggered by the whole thing. Maurice must have the keys then.'

At this point an office messenger knocked and entered with the day's paper. Hughes looked at it and frowned. He seemed to be looking at the front page for such a long time that Jenkins couldn't help asking, 'Anything wrong?'

Hughes tore his eyes away from the paper to tell him. 'A miner was killed in the mine, but it's believed he was murdered by his fellow miners who are members of a secret society,' said Hughes, proffering the paper.

'What?' exclaimed Jenkins, reaching for it. He began to read the account of the murder which was the lead story in the paper. 'Ephraim Obi, for seven years a miner, was on Saturday found dead at the pit head. His throat was slashed and he lay in a pool of blood. He was accidentally found by a group of boys hiking near the mines. Police are investigating.'

'Incredible!' exclaimed Jenkins, passing the paper back to Hughes. The phone began to ring again. Hughes picked up the receiver. 'Yes?'

'This is Bailey, sir. All the drivers have now returned to headquarters and reported that Maurice is nowhere to be found.' When Bailey felt that Hughes had digested this information, he went on, 'I telephoned Ukana as you instructed about letting the Chief know what's happening.' Bailey paused for breath and Hughes cut in. 'Well?' 'Well, sir,' continued Bailey, 'Mr Anako, the interpreter there, told me that the Chief had already sent someone to tell him to call on him. This happened before I telephoned him with your instructions.'

'I see,' said Hughes slowly. Jenkins watched Hughes' face as the latter hung up. In the same slow voice he told Jenkins, 'The drivers found no trace of Maurice.' But somehow, by accident or design, he failed to mention to the other man about the Chief's wish to see their man at Ukana. 'But where could Maurice have got to? How could he have vanished into thin air, and with four court messengers and a driver who knows the whole of the region like the back of his hand?' He looked perplexedly at Jenkins.

'He must have been after something big and very serious or he wouldn't have taken our best local staff with him.'

'I agree,' conceded Hughes. 'All the same, you might have thought that he'd leave word with someone. But no, he had to do it all by himself! Ever since his success, which I learned of from hearsay, at Ichara, the man has become difficult to handle. And not only by me ; my predecessors, I gather had their belly full of him as well. A little success, like a little education, is a very dangerous thing!'

Jenkins sucked in his lips and sat rigidly in his chair to stop himself from laughing. When he felt that he could safely speak without doing so, he told Hughes, 'I gathered from the night-watchman at Ukana that he heard a van start up there sometime during the night.'

'Oh?' Hughes asked, interested. His face looked hopeful.

'How true I don't know,' Jenkins added quickly, anxious not to raise the D.C.'s hopes too much on that score, in case it came to nothing.

'Go on,' Hughes urged, Jenkins's hesitancy or his doubts having not registered with him.

Jenkins cleared his throat and went on in the same doubtful voice. 'He's terribly old, the night-watchman I mean. I frankly don't know whether to believe his story or not, because he told me at first that he was napping when the keys were removed from his small shed. Later he mentioned the incident about the van.' He paused and continued with a touch of humour, 'I think he added the latter to make amends for napping on duty!'

Hughes grunted, and considered what Jenkins had just

told him. 'I don't know, Mark. Somehow I don't agree with your theory that the night-watchman invented that story merely to extricate himself from his dilemma. These old men are very good watchdogs, even though they nod off now and then. A whole family could go off to the market for the day and leave an army of children in the care of the aged member of the family, and return from the market late at night to find both home and children intact. Nothing has been burgled. You won't find a thief breaking into a home where he knows that there's an old man or woman stretched out somewhere on a mat, either asleep or watching. Thieves suspect all old people here of witchcraft.'

When Hughes had finished, Jenkins pointed out, 'He's the caretaker as well.'

'What? Can't they find someone else to take on the other job?'

'I don't know, that was surely MacIntosh's and now Maurice's affair.'

Hughes laid that matter aside for the moment. 'Look, Mark, if the night-watchman said he heard a noise, then he must have done.'

'I wouldn't attach too much importance to it,' warned Jenkins, but Hughes's mind was moving in another direction. 'If those keys were stolen as we originally thought, he would've heard the noise even though he was napping, and would've got up as they were being removed. Taking this fact into consideration, I feel positive that he heard a van start up,' Hughes said with conviction.

'Oh, George, we can't be sure. I told you he's very old,' Jenkins argued.

'I know, you've told me, and I've also told you about their resilience. There's something about them you won't find among our old at home. I don't know what it is that keeps them mentally alert here. I suppose, not being used to the comforts of life, the feather beds and the rest of it, discomfort keeps their minds working even if they doze off now and again. I'll have to look into his being a caretaker as well, unless he enjoys doing it.'

'He doesn't,' Jenkins informed him. 'I gather he finds it a bit much doing the two jobs at once.'

'I should say he does, sweeping and cleaning by day and watching at night!' he exclaimed and tapped his front tooth. 'Look, Mark, I want that night-watchman brought down here. I have my reasons, and if they're not already obvious to you, I want to interrogate him myself about the noise he heard.'

'But I've already done so,' said Jenkins, a little annoyed. 'I'm sure that if he'd something more to add, he'd have told me.'

Hughes ignored the annoyance in the other man. 'Hmm. Just the same, have him driven down in the van at Ukana. Pity Fenner's travelling up to the coast with MacIntosh. Bailey's too young and hopeless,' Hughes observed and paused for a moment as he smoothed his moustache. 'By the way, where's Underwood?' he asked.

'I expect he's around. Why? D'you want to see him?'

'Yes . . . I'll just give him a tinkle,' he added briskly and reached for the phone.

A few seconds later Bill Underwood walked in. Tall, fair and deeply tanned, he made both the District Commissioner and the Director of Information look like pale, scruffy ghosts. A sworn bachelor, he kept his appearances at the officers' club to a minimum, preferring the local bars in the township, where he found a more congenial atmosphere.

Hughes stared at him and blinked at the healthy look Underwood had, grudgingly conceding that he was also immensely handsome.

When Underwood had first arrived as Co-ordination Officer, the District Commissioner had been dubious about his ability and capacity for work because of his good looks. But the years, he was happy to say, had proved him wrong. The man's good looks were a secondary attribute. But what he did in the township in his free time, Hughes hardly dared think.

Hughes glanced briefly at the map of the British Isles on the right-hand side of his office wall as he began to speak to Underwood. Underwood, in turn, always found this habit of his senior official rather amusing. He had not quite been able to make out during the three years he had been there whether his presence irritated the man so much that he had to glance at the map before he spoke to him. Anyway, he had long since stopped worrying about it. And let his superior get on with whatever ailed him.

'I suppose you've heard that we're looking for Maurice?'

When Underwood nodded, Hughes went on, 'Mark here has just come back from Ukana and our drivers are also back from their various searching trips.' Hughes stopped and looked from Jenkins and back again to Underwood. 'One thing bothers me about all this. Maurice, with all his faults, and heaven alone knows they're legion, hasn't bothered to telephone in to tell us about his whereabouts. He would have done so in normal circumstances,' he said, emphasising the point by tapping his forefinger on the edge of his desk. 'As Mark rightly said earlier, he must have gone after something very big indeed, and hoped that he'd complete it quickly and be back in his office at the usual time. Now, gentlemen, I know that you'll perhaps think that I'm acting too hastily, and you'll be right in thinking that I see a man holding up a machete ready to strike behind every palm tree. I'm frankly not at all happy just sitting here and waiting for Maurice to turn up with the driver and our court messengers. I'm also inclined to believe that the night-watchman at Ukana heard a van starting up in the night.' He turned to Jenkins. 'Phone Ukana directly after you leave here and tell them to send the night-watchman to me.' He paused and looked out of the window on his left as he continued, 'What I propose to do is this. I want you, Bill, to drive up to Ukana and when you get there, see whether there are tyre marks on the road entering the township. I know there's only one true main road, the rest are bicycle tracks.'

Jenkins spoke up, 'That may prove impossible. Dust and foot marks would have obliterated what chance there is of finding anything. We know what they can do on roads.'

'We'll do the impossible. We'll look hard to find what we want to find. The rains haven't started yet, which is a bit of luck on our side.'

'Heavy lorries carrying traders also go into the village, George,' Jenkins pointed out.

'I know they do, but the tyres of a van are much smaller than those of the lorries,' contradicted Hughes.

'Jeeps and kit cars?' Jenkins asked.

'What about them?' Hughes echoed. 'Anyway their tyres are also bigger.'

Jenkins looked defeated. 'I see,' he said, and sat well back in his chair.

Underwood looked from Hughes to Jenkins to see

whether they had finished their exchanges. 'D'you want me to leave immediately?' he asked at last.

'Yes,' Hughes replied, and then asked Jenkins, 'Anyone there you think might give him a hand?'

'Only Mr Anako, the interpreter.'

Hughes was absorbed for a while. 'Take Bailey with you, Bill, that'd give him something to do, as well as keep him out of mischief!'

Jenkins and Underwood left the District Commissioner's office.

'Eze you finish chop?'

'Yes, Mr Anako,' answered the night-watchman, who had been to his home for lunch and back.

'You know say you no for lef for go chop until two o'clock?'

'I know, but Mr Anako, I be ol' man and my belly rumble. Beside, court no sit today. I no bin get nothing for do,' he explained.

'For which place be driver?' the court interpreter inquired as he looked around.

'I think he be inside garage. I see him go there when I come back for sit under window.'

'I hear from headquarter now-now. They say they want make you and the driver for go there.'

Eze rose to his feet with a start. 'Eh? What them want?' he asked hysterically.

Anako looked at him irritably. 'How I go know? How I go stay for Ukana and know what happen for Utuka?' he asked back.

'For which time they want make we come?' the night-watchman asked again when he was able to control the tremor in his voice. But Anako had seen the fear in Eze's face and so he asked, 'What worry you?'

'Nothing!' shouted Eze in an unnatural voice. 'I jus' want for know what they want me for the place. I no leave this township before for go any other place for my life,' he explained.

Anako considered this and then told Eze, 'Me no know the reason why they want you myself. It mean I no go fit go now for see Chief Obieze until you come back. I get message for him from Mr. Bailey, and Chief himself want to see me,' Anako said, perplexed.

Eze's ears pricked up at these pieces of information. They might be useful to him in his new role as an informer, he thought. His recent fears about being summoned to headquarters vanished. He saw it now as a further means of obtaining more information.

'Well, what you wait for?' Anako broke into Eze's thoughts to inquire. Eze started, and cleared his throat. A faint smile touched the corners of his mouth. 'I go-go one-time for tell driver!' and left.

Anako watched with amazement the sudden spring that came into the old night-watchman's feet. 'Wonder no go cease!' he shouted into the hot and humid afternoon air, and went about his business. As Eze and the driver drove past him on their way to Utuka, Anako watched enviously as he'd never been to headquarters himself.

Underwood and Bailey passed the van at Ujo River. As the hanging bridge over the river could take only one vehicle at a time, Underwood, at the wheel of his own car, had to give way to the oncoming van at the foot of the bridge, hoping that there was no other approaching traffic behind it. Sometimes a motorist could be delayed at the foot of the bridge for nearly an hour.

As the van drew nearer, Bailey nudged Underwood. 'That's one of ours,' he said, pointing with his chin. They watched as the van drew parallel to them. Underwood at once recognised them and inclined his head in greeting them. He had met them at the sub-station some months before MacIntosh took over. They, in turn, acknowledged his greeting and drove past.

'They're our men,' he told Bailey.

'Where could they be heading for?' Bailey asked. Underwood, who was now driving on the bridge, didn't reply immediately as he was manipulating his car through a tricky part of the hanging bridge. 'George asked Mark to telephone for the night-watchman to go down and see him,' he explained later.

Satisfied, Bailey looked about him. 'I say, Bill, what a delightful sight this is!'

'The hills you mean?' Underwood asked, without taking his eyes away from the bridge planks.

When Bailey murmured a reply, Underwood went on to enlighten him. 'They're the famous hills of Ukana.' He quickly took his eyes away from the bridge and saw the mirrored surprise on Bailey's face. 'Haven't you been this way before?' Underwood asked him.

'No. I've been to Idom, of course, and to Ule, but not here. The scenery is magnificent!' he added ecstatically. He watched with wonder as young boys and girls, from the age of about seven to fourteen, dived into the river from the over-hanging rocks on both sides, disappearing for seconds, and then emerging and disappearing again as if they were part of the river, and were merely surfacing at intervals to see the other world.

Bailey reluctantly tore his eyes away from them to look ahead. The bridge was over half a mile long, and when it was built it was proclaimed the longest bridge in the region. Underwood, clear of it now, changed into first gear to take them up the hill. On both sides of the road were women nursing tiny fires on which they warmed large clay pots filled with black-eyed beans, boiled yams, a variety of soups and boiled rice. They hoped lorry drivers and their loads of traders might stop or be stranded there for hours with failed brakes or flat tyres.

'I suggest you put your window up or we'll be covered with red dust,' Underwood advised Bailey.

'As bad as that?' Bailey asked, winding up his window.

'Hmm. I remember travelling this way once with George who's a fresh air fiend. I was new up here then, and was so angry when I reached home and saw the damage the dust had done. For weeks afterwards the white shirt and shorts I wore on the memorable trip remained pink. The earth here doesn't wash out when it gets on white things.'

Bailey, who had been half listening, murmured, 'I love this part. You could say it's love at first sight.'

'It's all right,' shrugged Underwood, 'but I wouldn't like to find myself in its sub-station. I'd go mad. It's the loneliest place in the world, in fact all the sub-stations are lonely.' He changed gear and added jokingly, 'I think all the expatriate bungalows in the sub-stations should be called individually *Hermit's Wake*!'

44

Bailey laughed and became serious again. 'I really mean it, Bill. I'd love to live in this area.'

'But you're already living in this area,' Underwood reminded him. 'However, if you mean you'd particularly like to live in Ukana, I'll put a word in for you.'

Bailey's eyes gleamed as he turned his head and looked at Underwood.

'D'you really mean that, Bill?' he asked. 'Would you really do that for me?'

Another MacIntosh, thought Underwood privately. Another one with a burning zeal. Aloud he told his passenger, 'I don't appoint people to posts. My putting in a good word for you wasn't meant seriously, and there's Oliver Fenner and one or two others ahead of you in the race,' Underwood told him, not wishing to be involved.

Bailey sat back in his seat. 'Oh yes, of course. I'd forgotten that,' he replied and a light went from his eyes.

'For which place you think the people we jus' pass want for go?' Eze asked the driver as they travelled in the opposite direction.

'That be Mr Underwood we pass and another man. I no know for which place they go. Maybe they go for Umuora or Ukana, I no fit say.'

'Ah, Odu, the worl' big!' exclaimed the toothless Eze as his eyes feasted on the new vista that lay about him. 'This be first time I lef Ukana. I no know say worl' big so!'

The knowledgeable and much travelled Odu agreed with him. 'Make you wait first until you see Utuka,' said Odu. 'The place fine. Utuka get fine township, fine womans. For two-pence hapney you fit lie on top one womans until you tire!'

'Eh?' Eze asked, incredulous. He counted himself now as a member of the middle class. With the assurance of another pound a month from his sideline activity for *The Daily Observer*, together with his salary of seven shillings and six-pence, he was wealthy.

His throat grew tight with anticipation. It was a long time since he'd had a woman, not since his wife died. And after that, what women there were he couldn't afford on his meagre salary. But now fate had stepped in, as it often did unexpectedly, to calm troubled waters, and smooth rugged paths. Now he could afford them *en masse*: those that had looked at him before, but had shaken their heads because he hadn't any money; and others who hadn't looked at him at all. He looked forward now to one of life's greatest pleasures with feverish hope.

The driver seemed to have divined Eze's thoughts for he told him, 'But you no get strength to sleep with womans now eh, pa? Your limp weak!'

'Ah! But that no mean to say my thing weak!' chortled Eze.

Odu braked and stopped. He gave Eze a sidelong glance and burst out laughing. He started up the van again, still smiling, and observed, 'Which womans go want old man like you?'

Eze patted the pound hidden in his loin cloth and smiled at Odu with confidence. 'Make you no worry for that. Make you jus' keep your eye for road!' And the driver did just that.

When they arrived at the government offices at Utuka, it was already past two, and the offices were closed for the day. They hung about perplexed. Finally an office messenger who was still lingering around directed them to Hughes's home.

'Hey!' Odu shouted. Hughes's steward, hurriedly descending the back stairs that led to the kitchen, turned. 'What you want?' he asked.

'D.C.,' replied Odu. 'We come from Ukana.'

At this juncture Eze felt himself chiefly concerned in this matter and took over from Odu. 'D.C. want for see me, he say so himself this morning-time. The driver here bring me come.'

'I see,' the steward replied. 'Make you wait for here. I go-go tell him.'

Seconds later the steward returned to inform them, 'D.C. say make you wait small.'

The newcomers nodded and went to lean against their van.

'Well, this is Ukana, ancient town of red earth and so on,' said Underwood getting out of the car which he had parked at the beginning of the main road that led into the township. 'You know what we're supposed to look for?' he asked Bailey.

Bailey registered his surprise. 'No, I didn't know we came to look for something, I thought we merely came to cast our eyes over the native court as MacIntosh and Maurice are both away.'

Underwood's eyebrows rose perceptibly. 'My dear boy, we're here to look for tyre marks!'

Bailey's mouth hung open, he swallowed and asked, 'What tyre marks?'

'Van tyre marks to be exact. Didn't George tell you?' When Bailey shook his head, Underwood enlarged. 'I thought you knew before we left Utuka.'

'No. No one told me anything.'

'Well, you know now!' Underwood told him.

Bailey, who stood with his hands resting on his hips, inquired with shock, 'You mean we're about to trace what might be Maurice's route?'

'Yes, that sort of thing.'

'But all the sub-stations I contacted this morning reported not having seen him. I mean, I know he was here last week, but he'd since returned to headquarters.'

Underwood agreed but briefed him more. 'We've since learned that the night-watchman from here, and by the way he was one of the two we met in the van at Ujo River, heard a van start up here last night.'

'What?' asked Bailey, moving closer to Underwood. 'And you think that Maurice was in the van that started up?'

Underwood sighed. 'I don't know, the whole thing is merely a supposition, to me at any rate, but George thinks differently. Anyway, we don't want to leave any stone unturned.'

'I see.'

'Good. Now will you bend down as I'm doing and help me look for the marks?'

'The D.C. want for see you now,' Hughes's steward informed Eze and Odu.

'You mean he want see me, or he want see me and driver?' Eze asked to make quite sure that the steward had not misrepresented Hughes's words.

The steward looked staggered and uncertain. He made as

if to go back and ask Hughes exactly what he meant, but changed his mind as he feared his employer's reaction. To save his own skin he simply repeated what he'd told them before, and quickly ran down the stairs into the kitchen.

Eze wobbled forward. The long drive from Ukana seemed to have tired him out. He waved Odu, who was about to follow in his wake, to a halt. 'I think I go fit manage with D.C.!' he told him, smirking. Odu opened his mouth to protest but shut it again, overwhelmed with surprise.

'I be the night-watchman you send for see, sir!' Eze announced as he stood facing Hughes on the verandah.

'So you're the man with the double responsibility?' Hughes inquired slightly amused.

'Yes, sir,' he replied, having no idea what Hughes meant, but he reckoned that as the D.C. was smiling, there couldn't be much wrong in just saying yes.

'You definitely heard a van start up last night as you told Mr Jenkins?'

The words van and Jenkins registered immediately. 'Yes, sir, I hear van with my own ear!'

'Did you see it?'

'No, sir, but I hear it!' Eze replied in the same loud voice as if daring Hughes to dispute it.

'Are you sure of it?'

'I sure, master!' replied Eze earnestly.

If there had been some doubt in Hughes's mind, there was none now as he looked at Eze with searching penetration. 'All right,' Hughes said. 'About what time of night did you hear the noise?'

'It no be for night-time, it be for early, early this morning-time.'

'But you told Mr Jenkins it was at night that you heard the noise,' Hughes reminded him.

'Yes, sir,' Eze agreed, and went on to explain. 'It still be dark, but it be early morning. Sun no come yet, and bird no start for cry.'

Hughes nodded comprehendingly. 'Oh I see, towards dawn.'

Eze replied excitedly, 'Ah, master, you talk true word!'

'Are you quite certain that the noise you heard wasn't made by a lorry travelling on the main road? The native court premises at Ukana are near the main road you know,'

'I know, master. Before, me self bin think noise come from road but I certain now noise come from inside native courtyard,' said Eze vehemently.

Hughes said nothing for a while. 'I see. Is that the driver from Ukana over there?' he asked.

'Yes, sir, but he no know anything about this palaver!' Eze hastily informed him, reluctant to share the limelight with Odu.

'I still would like to speak to him.'

A defeated look came to Eze's face as he yielded to the District Commissioner's request. 'All right, sir, I go call him come.' He turned and beckoned to Odu.

'How long have you been the driver for the sub-station?' Hughes asked Odu as the latter drew nearer.

'Three year.'

'Did you go anywhere with the van during the early hours of this morning? Or see anyone on the premises?'

'No, sir, I no go any place and I no see nothing.'

Hughes turned once more to the nightwatchman. 'How much pay d'you receive from holding down two jobs?'

'Seven shilling sixpence,' Eze told him, taken by surprise.

'We'll make it up to fifteen shillings, but only for your services as a night-watchman. We'll get someone else as janitor. How does that sound?'

Eze thanked him effusively, but kept his own counsel.

'You may go back to Ukana now.'

'Yes, sir,' they chorused and left.

Back in the car and out of the residential area of govern-ment officials, the now affluent and flushed Eze inquired, 'For which place you say all the womans be?'

Odu pressed his foot hard on the accelerator. 'I no know. We go back to Ukana!' he grumbled.

Eze caught the point but didn't help the situation by giggling as he asked the driver, 'You vex with me because you yourself no get increment from D.C.?'

'Ah, Frederick!' shouted Odu, addressing the recently chistened night-watchman by his christian name. 'That no be for here or for there. I just want get home quick,' he said irritably.

'But you bin say . . .'

'Shut your mouth!' interrupted Odu angrily, 'or I go put you down here for waka waka go reach Ukana!'

The night-watchman sat back in his seat without making another sound.

'D'you think this is really necessary?' Bailey inquired of Underwood after they'd been bending for some yards.

'Afraid so,' muttered Underwood and swore under his breath. He too was beginning to hate their mission which seemed pointless to him.

'How far does this road go?'

'Heaven alone knows. It could go as far as eternity for all I know. I've never been on it before,' he said and stood up to stretch. Bailey followed his example. His eyes caught some wild fruit hanging tantalisingly from bent branches. 'Are those edible d'you know?'

'Are what edible?' Underwood asked, as his eyes followed to where Bailey was pointing. 'No, they're called dog's-what-not. My cook told me. I nearly had a go at some when I first arrived, but he rescued me just in time.'

'They look awfully good.'

'Yes. When opened they contain a sort of milky liquid.'

Bailey brought his attention back to their task. 'There's loads of bicycle marks but none of lorries,' he observed.

'If you ask me I think our best bet is to get back into the car and drive very slowly with our eyes wide open. I've had quite enough of this bending,' Underwood moaned as he straightened up.

'Ditto here.'

'George, what's it all about? You were very distracted all through the meal,' said Mrs Hughes, as they sipped their after-lunch coffee.

Hughes eyed her from the rim of his coffee cup. 'What d'you mean?'

'Those men you were speaking to on the verandah a short while ago.'

Hughes sipped his coffee. 'They're from Ukana.'

'Where that fellow MacIntosh was?'

'Yes, Millie, where that fellow MacIntosh was,' Hughes cruelly mimicked.

'Anything wrong?' Millicent Hughes pressed on, ignoring her husband's insult. She was a capable woman with an attractive personality, but unfortunately her husband never allowed her head to rise above water.

Hughes's brows jiggled as he replied, 'Wrong? That's an understatement – Maurice has disappeared!'

'What?' cup and saucer rattling in her hand.

'Yes, or so it appears.'

'Since when?' she asked, first depositing her best china safely on a small side table, her dark eyes intent on her husband.

'For God's safe, Millie! Must I go over it all again at home?'

'Well, dear, you know you never tell me anything unless I ask.'

Hughes turned towards her and at the same time cut her short. 'All right, dear! Maurice didn't turn up in the office all day. He isn't sick at home – no one knows where he is, and neither does anyone know at the sub-stations.'

Mrs Hughes pinched her lower lip. 'Oh dear! You don't think . . .'

'That he's been eaten up by a wild beast?' Hughes interjected. 'I doubt it.' Not waiting for his wife's reply he continued, 'Maurice's much too agile and experienced for that sort of thing to happen to him. At least I hope he is!'

Seeing the anxiety on her husband's face, Mrs Hughes said encouragingly, 'He may still turn up. It's only just past three.'

Hughes glanced at his watch to double check. 'I sincerely hope so, or I wouldn't know how to begin to explain, or what to explain!'

'George, dear, do be careful.'

'I don't care!' he snapped.

Millicent Hughes stared at him. 'Aren't you worrying rather unnecessarily?' she asked.

He swung round in his chair to face her once more. As he did so he caught what seemed to be a look of secret enjoyment on her face. It was as if she was enjoying his dilemma, but at the same time trying to cover up by being solicitous. He chose to ignore it. As he sat back in his chair something seemed to break in him. He decided that, laugh at him or not, he needed her support now more than he had ever imagined he would. After all, who else was there to turn to?

'Worry?' he said, 'that's putting it mildly, my dear. I'm frightened, Millie, terribly frightened. I've never had this feeling come over me before that something tragic has happened.'

'But surely it's only today that he's been missed?' contributed Mrs Hughes, jollying her husband along. He's worried and he needs me. The scoundrel, she thought.

'That doesn't lessen my anxiety,' Hughes replied, and paused. 'I may be wrong as you say, and he may yet turn up.' He paused again. 'Oh I don't know, my cup is certainly full and running over!'

'I suggest you have your usual afternoon nap. I'm sure by tea time things will have resolved themselves,' she said in a pacifying tone which, to Hughes's sharp ears, sounded false.

'How?' asked Hughes, hoping his wife would come up with a solution. Instead she told him, 'You can't do much about it by worrying.'

He again assumed his patronising attitude. 'Millie, I don't think you've grasped the situation. I dispatched a man home only yesterday, and I can't find another today. The Governor will begin to wonder what's the matter with me.'

'Thank heavens we're retiring next year,' she said softly and with relief.

'That's not the way to look at it, and it isn't quite what I meant. We may not see next year here. Knowing the Governor as I do, he may just let things mark time here temporarily while he asks the Colonial Office to retire me. Then a new man will take over. It would be a disgraceful end to a long and brilliant career!'

'Good!' Mrs Hughes let fall without thinking. 'I didn't mean it that way,' she said contritely. 'I think I'll join you after all in a short nap,' she added, but hoped he wouldn't accept her offer.

He looked at her for a long time, and his reply when it came soothed her ears. 'No, dear, I'll wait up in case something turns up. I sent Underwood and Bailey to Ukana. I should hate to be caught napping when they return. It's hardly the example to set to one's juniors.'

Mrs Hughes made no reply. She went into their bedroom and closed the door. Hughes watched her go and then picked

52

up an old copy of the *Tatler* and restlessly put it down again. But as he did so a photograph of a large pin-up, his one unsuspected vicarious pleasure, slid out and fell on the carpet. He picked it up quickly and looked about him frantically. How could he have mislaid it there? Had Millie seen it? He normally hid them in his study. Then he remembered. He'd been looking at this, with some others, in his study only yesterday afternoon. He'd glanced up briefly to see Maurice's car approaching and thought that Maurice was coming to call on him to tell him about MacIntosh's departure. He had hastily shoved the pictures into a drawer and locked it, but in his haste one did not go in with the rest, so he had put it into the nearest thing he could lay his hands on, and dashed from his study to meet Maurice. Before he had reached the verandah it was obvious that Maurice had not intended calling on him, but was heading for the club. He then strolled around on his front lawn, but by the time he got back to the lounge, he had forgotten all about the picture. All he saw in his hand was the *Tatler* and wondered what on earth he was doing with it, and so he put it on the coffee table and thought no more of it. Sweat sprang behind his moustache and his usual pretentious manner deserted him. He glanced at their bedroom door uncertainly. Should he go in and join his wife to see what he could glean from her behaviour towards him, or should he stay and act as if nothing had happened?

Without thinking, and before he could solve his problem, his feet shuffled like a murderer revisiting the scene of his crime towards their bedroom. He tapped lightly on the door. 'Millie, are you asleep?'

'No, why?' Mrs Hughes shouted from behind the closed door.

His heart sank. 'I merely asked, dear,' he replied and twisted the door knob.

Mrs Hughes was standing beside her bed in her pants and nothing else, and for the life of him Hughes could not tell from the way she was looking at him daringly whether she was going to beat him, or was merely trying to prove that she was just as endowed as his little tart in the picture. He found himself comparing the two. The vision of loveliness between the pages of the *Tatler*, and his wife of thirty years. He shuddered. 'Perish the thought!' he muttered, and

53

started as his wife said, 'What's the matter with you, George?'

Hughes recovered himself and squared his jaw. 'Nothing. Should there be?'

'That's what I'd like to know,' she replied, brushing back her auburn hair which was now flecked with grey.

'Oh, God!' he moaned and fled from the room. How long has Millicent known that I've these sort of pictures? he asked himself over and over again. And yet she'd made me feel that I was the dominant figure in the house. He answered the question himself. Only a woman who had ceased to care and inwardly despised her husband, would turn her back and leave him to stumble along in his fools' paradise, and hope that he managed to break his neck in the process!

He stopped pacing to wipe the perspiration from his face. His clammy hands picked up the magazine again. 'Fool, fool, fool!' he cried. 'So that's why she shoved me out of the double bed into a single one, on the pretext that the climate was too hot to sleep in a double. And fool that I am I believed her.' He sighed, not knowing which way to turn. He took out the photograph and began to tear it to pieces, muttering to himself as he did so. 'She's always had it over me,' he continued to mutter. 'In the most important things in life she's always had it over me despite all my outward show of strength. Real strength lies within.' He sighed and collapsed on to the sofa and undid his tie.

Chapter Five

The offices of *The Daily Observer* were at Amaku, forty odd miles east of Utuka and fifteen miles west of Ukana. Amaku had been a thriving town of petty trading, brewing of illicit gin and farming before the arrival of heavy industries and Barclays Bank. In no other town in the region was there more colour, noise and people to be found than there. The town always made a marked impression on visitors with her huge market where people would congregate like a swarm of locusts, fights occurring between traders and customers if the latter suspected that they had been gypped, however minutely.

But more important than all these, Amaku, to her natural inhabitants, was a town they loved and understood: an African township, pure and simple.

Things might have stayed that way but for the arrival of foreign investors and the industrial complexities they created. The townspeople, though aware from the outset that these strange bed-fellows had arrived, nevertheless wore a look of perpetual surprise at the whole idea. In time, for want of nothing else to do, and with the feeling of what can not be helped must be endured, the two communities formed an uneasy alliance. If the mass took this unease in their stride, it was a different matter with the town elders who, having waxed fat through cunning, nepotic practices and playing on the general apathy and ignorance of those they represented, resented the intrusion. They particularly feared that the managers of the new industries would increase wages to unbelievable heights and therefore give stature as well as a voice to a hitherto pliable and sleepy mass, with the result that they would find themselves swept out of power and be replaced by a more aggressive and volatile group.

Besides the worried elders were other groups of people who were the élite and who in turn had nothing but contempt for the elders who conducted the affairs of Amaku. The latter formed a clique and liked nothing better than to spend their evenings at each other's homes, splicing the rounds of brandy and soda with fond recollections of their student days in lodgings in Fulham, Camden Town and Notting Hill Gate, and of their Sunday afternoons in Hyde Park listening to the speakers on their soap boxes.

The town elders had no time for the *Observer*. It poked not only its nose into, but also meddled in the affairs that were of no concern to them. The élite, on the other hand, read the 'scandal sheets' as they referred to the paper, condescendingly. It was not *The Times* of course, but it would fill in the gap until *The Times* surface mail edition arrived.

The town's representatives still smarted from the rebuke in a front page editorial that called them 'wasteful men'.

They proposed to build a new meeting hall that befitted the rising Amaku instead of, as the paper suggested, using the money to re-roof a leaking school that stood in danger of collapsing on to the heads of children, with the coming of the rainy season.

As these two groups, the élite and the elders, or representatives, to use a modern term, had no time for the *Observer*, so the paper set out to cut them down to fractional size! But more important, it unleased its prodigious influence to educate the masses, and the masses, in turn and in gratitude, drank in the written words in all its pages, lustily.

Progress and awareness had arrived and they could no more be halted than could the sources of the Niger or the Zambezi. While those who made it their business to hold the tide back adopted the attitude of 'wait, you go see ; they go tire', the paper, like a voice in the wilderness propagated its many themes : TELL THE PEOPLE THE TRUTH ; THE DIGNITY OF MAN – THE MASSES ; A SPEEDY PROGRESS TO SELF-RULE. The last theme made government officials cringe, and their attitude to this onslaught was one of contempt and suspicion.

And it came about that on the afternoon that Mason's would-be route was being investigated by Underwood and the junior secretary, Bailey, the elders of Amaku were locked in a meeting that had dissolved into a cut-throat battle. Yet they were determined that it should not be adjourned again, as it had been three times already, without resolving a decision on the apportioning of market stalls. So heated was the debate, with a decision at last within grasp, that they missed the fleeting face and hand that appeared and vanished within seconds from one of the windows of the meeting hall – the hand propelling a free copy of the *Observer* through the window lattice.

The strange hiss and splash, seemingly coming from nowhere until it reached the floor, silenced the voices in the debating chamber, and brought all the members' eyes round to where the noise came from. In all the history of their meeting hall it was such an unnatural thing to happen that they sat paralysed and stunned. Finally their rotund chairman, Julius Anyaeze, got up and hurried to pick up the paper. He looked at the front page and then held it up for the others to see. FOUL PLAY SUSPECTED IN MINE DEATH! screamed the headline. The meeting broke up.

'I think make we stop for get chop. I hungry,' Eze told Odu when they reached Ujo River from Utuka.

'I no get money. It be middle of month, all my money finish,' Odu replied.

'It no matter, I go pay,' Eze assured him. Odu almost ran the van into the river, so great was his shock.

'From which place you get the money? Your pay small pass my own,' he reminded Eze.

'Make you no worry for that!' snapped Eze, and asked him pointedly, 'You want chop or you no want chop?'

'Ah, I want chop,' the driver replied, still shocked at the offer of a meal from the night-watchman. He crossed the bridge and pulled clear of the main road.

'We're nearly entering the town; I suppose it's the town, and we've not seen any tyre marks,' Underwood complained.

'True. D'you suppose we'll find any?' Bailey asked.

'I don't know. As far as I'm concerned this pursuit is a wild goose chase, but let it not be said that we shirked our duty. It's a good thing that we're not meeting any other vehicles or our ears would be red from abuse by now!' commented Underwood.

'Can we go into the town?'

'For what?'

'Oh nothing. I'm just curious.'

'Not today, I'm afraid, we've got to get back to report to George. Knowing him, I'm sure he's already stamping his feet waiting for us.'

'Wait! Reverse back a little!' Bailey shouted. 'I think I saw a streak of marks!'

'Where?' asked Underwood, looking about him from one end of the road to the other.

'Just pull back a yard or so.'

Underwood reversed and stopped. They looked and then jumped out to have a closer look.

'Are you sure they weren't made by us?' Underwood inquired as both men slammed their doors.

'Positive. I saw the marks before we first went over them.'

They inspected the marks. 'They look to me as if they were

57

made when a car stopped suddenly,' observed Underwood, with a professional eye.

'That must be it then!' exclaimed Bailey with glee.

But Underwood warned him, 'Let's not jump ahead of ourselves! They may not be the ones we're looking for.'

'But we've seen no others since we started,' Bailey reminded him.

'True, still we must be certain.' As he straightened up he further suggested, 'I think we should drive a bit more to see whether there're any more.' Before they got back in the car Underwood told Bailey, 'It seems you're right. The marks we've just seen are almost certainly those of a van. I suggest, though, that we put stones to mark the spot so as not to risk going past it on our way back.'

Eze licked the last drop of soup in the enamel bowl and turned to the driver. 'If you finish chop I think we start for go.' The driver agreed and they both went down to the river to wash their hands. They drove into the grounds of the native court, Ukana, as the court interpreter was getting up from the stool under MacIntosh's office window to stretch his legs.

Eze was convulsed with laughter as he beheld the dignified Anako doing the same exercises as he did after long periods of sitting still, watching the premises. He couldn't resist a little thrust. 'You see how the job hard, Mr Anako?'

Anako ignored him. 'Well, what happen for headquarter then?'

'Make you ask Eze,' Odu told him. 'He go first for talk with D.C., and D.C. give him increment!'

'Eh!' shouted Anako, round-eyed.

Eze nodded with satisfaction as he confirmed it. 'That be so. I go get fifteen shilling for every month, and D.C. also tell me say another man go do all the dirty janitor work!'

Anako stared at him speechless.

'I think make you begin for find another janitor, Mr Anako,' Eze went on. 'I no think say I go be able for do the two job tomorrow,' he warned.

'But for which place I go find man now-now? Evening-time soon come. This place quiet for evening-time,' Anako remonstrated.

Eze reacted as if he couldn't care less. 'Me self no know,

58

all I know be say I no go fit do janitor work tomorrow morning.'

The court interpreter suddenly became angry. 'If you lef the janitor work before I find another man, I go tell Mr Jenkin say make he sack you!' he threatened.

That brought the night-watchman back to his senses. 'All right, all right!' he said soothingly. 'I go do the work, but make you find somebody quick, Mr Anako!'

'So what happen for Utuka?' Anako asked, after their differences were solved.

'The D.C. want for hear with him own ear the same thing I bin tell you and Mr Jenkin this morning-time.'

'Ah,' murmured Anako with relief. 'I see. Well, since you and Odu be here now, I think I go-go now to see what Chief Obieze want.'

He went home to fetch his bicycle and then left.

As he neared the town, Underwood stopped the car because he had recognised the face approaching them. Anako quickly braked and walked over to the car.

'Mr Underwood! I no know say, you come to Ukana!' Anako exclaimed with pleasure. Underwood, who spoke pidgin, smiled back and asked, 'How everything go for Ukana?'

Anako scratched his head and wiped his eyes. 'Things no good at all, Mr Underwood. Office lock, and we no fit find the key. Mr MacIntosh go leave, and no tell me before he go. And Mr Mason no come for take charge.'

Poor man, thought Underwood. 'This be Mr Bailey.'

'Ah, Mr Bailey! I bin talk with him for phone for this morning-time,' Anako said, grinning. Bailey smiled in return and shook hands.

'Which place you go now?' Underwood continued in fluent pidgin.

'I get message from headquarter, from Mr Bailey here, say, make I go tell Chief say, court lock and no go be for session because they want paint building. And Chief himself send word say, he want see me also.'

The smile vanished from Underwood's face. 'Oh, why he want to see you?'

'Me no know, Mr Underwood.'

'Chief always send word all the time for make you see him?' Underwood asked in a worried voice.

Anako caught his mood. 'Some time,' he said looking a

bit tired now, 'but not all the time. I think he been send word to me only one time, that be when his father die. Make you no forget say, he be new Chief. But whether he be new Chief or he no be new Chief, they no like for make friend with anybody way be in foreigner business.'

Underwood and Bailey nodded understandingly. 'I see,' Underwood replied almost inaudibly. 'They no like you because they think you go tell headquarters them secrets?'

'That be so, sir!'

'Well, make you no tell them headquarters secrets also!' Underwood advised him, and the three laughed.

'You go now for native court? If you go, and fit wait small there, I go finish with Chief quick and come meet you there.'

'No, Mr Anako, we drive back now to Utuka.'

Bailey cut in softly, 'Why not tell him what we've just seen?'

'No, we'll discuss it first with George. Mr Anako will be told in time,' Underwood replied, equally quietly.

'What say, sir?' Anako asked as he thought he heard his name mentioned.

'Oh, nothing. I just talk to Mr Bailey. By the way, Mr Anako,' Underwood continued as he suddenly remembered something, 'Mr Mason get the keys, that be the reason why native court lock.'

'Ah, I see,' replied the court interpreter with relief.

'But make you no tell Chief that!' Underwood warned him without knowing the reason why he did.

Anako shook his head vehemently as if to shake away such a horrible thought. 'Ah, no, I no go tell him,' he replied. 'But for which place Mr District Officer be?' he asked.

'He go for trek, Mr Anako,' Underwood told him, and started the car. An exchange of waves from the three, and the court interpreter remounted his bicycle and rode to his mission.

When they were well away from the spot Bailey turned to ask Underwood, 'Why didn't you tell him the truth about Maurice?'

'The truth?' Underwood asked back, changing gear. 'We don't know the truth ourselves!'

'But surely the tyre marks we've just seen and confirmed . . . and Maurice nowhere to be found as well . . .?'

'That doesn't mean that two and two always make four!'
Underwood cut in.

'No, even though they're supposed to. However, I still
think you should've told him that Maurice is nowhere to
be found. He looked to me a pretty honest fellow . . .'

'Honest he most certainly is,' Underwood interrupted
again to say, 'but I don't think we should tell all and sundry
our findings until we've discussed them with George. I don't
know how much he's guessed himself, the interpreter, I
mean. They're pretty astute. I'd much rather George asked
us to tell him.'

'I see.'

'Good!' interjected Underwood, and went on to recap
their activities of the afternoon aloud. 'We say three heavy
marks which looked as if they were made by a van when it
braked suddenly, two earlier on and another beside a
crooked palm tree quite near the town, right?'

'Right,' agreed Bailey.

'We drove a little further on without actually entering the
town to see if there were more, right? But there weren't.'

'Right.'

'In other words, mission accomplished!'

'Yes,' Bailey replied and looked at his watch. 'Half past
five! I'd have sworn it was less.'

'The sun often makes time deceptive here,' Underwood
replied as he braked at the junction where the main
thoroughfare crossed.

'I've never seen the native court before. Why don't we just
drop in for a second?' Bailey pleaded. 'I'm dying for a look.'

'When it's in session, it's most interesting. The sea of faces
and the noise – it often reminds me of the weekly market at
home. There's no point in going in when it's locked and no
one about.' He glanced briefly at Bailey and saw the look of
disappointment on his face. 'All right, just to satisfy your
curiosity, we'll take a quick look.'

The court interpreter cycled up to the Chief's compound
which stood on nearly fifteen acres of ground, was walled
in with red mortar six inches thick, and covered with corru-
gated iron. Goats, sheep and fowl roamed about freely as he
went through the gate. On his right more than two dozen
well-looked-after pigs snorted in their sty. He looked back at

the huge mahogany gate seven feet high and ten feet wide, with its fine carvings of favourite idols bending over sacrificial lambs. Satisfied, he continued on his journey. The gate was never shut except in time of war. On either side of him as he went were rows of thatched houses, the homes of the Chief's wives.

One outstanding feature that often strikes a visitor on entering the compound for the first time, is the residence of the Chief himself. It towers over all the other homes and gives the impression of being suspended in the air until, if by a stroke of luck, one happens to be present when the small discreet gate leading to the sanctum creaks slightly open to admit a distinguished guest, and the heavy concrete stilts on which the sanctum rests, are revealed. If, on the other hand, Divine providence had provided by accident of birth for you to come and go through that discreet gate at will, and it doesn't matter how many times you've done so, there's always a feeling of awe, coupled with a shuddering sensation. It's no wonder, for on the ground on which the Chief's home stood, deceased Chiefs have been buried for centuries, and powerful medicines are brewed. The walls of his home, if they had ears, must have listened to a thousand secret plots, about who shall be done away with, having become a potential danger to the community ; who should be sold into slavery to swell the exchequer, or who should be offered to the gods as an appeasement, an unfortunate act which would thenceforth render to his entire family the social stigma of 'outcasts'.

Anako knew these customs. He also knew that as soon as he had cycled out from the grounds of the native court to keep his appointment, informers had already whispered to the Chief that the court interpreter was on his way, and that news of his progress to the compound was reported every minute on the minute into the august ears of the exalted one.

By the time Anako had dismounted and leaned his bicycle on the wall beside the gate, Chief Obieze was already seated in his easy chair in the audience chamber to watch Anako progress across the vast span to reach him.

This is always an awe-inspiring and unnerving moment for anyone. For a missionary on his way to seek permission to build a church with a school attached, it is more than a nightmare, as he doesn't quite know how he will be received ;

in fact whether he will reach the august presence at all, not to mention from which direction a well-aimed arrow might spring. It is an unforgettable experience.

Chief Obieze eyed the court interpreter as the latter approached.

'I hear say they close native court. Why they close him, eh?' Obieze shouted before Anako got near him.

The court interpreter said nothing however until he stood before Obieze. He then ceremoniously bowed before he replied. 'They want for paint court.'

'Eh?' Obieze shouted. 'But who paint court or any place before rain come?' he asked, and answered the question himself. 'Nobody do that kind of thing for this country! For this region!'

'That be so, Chief.'

'So?'

Anako swallowed hard. 'I no fit say what I no know, Chief. Mr District Commissioner sent word for tell you say him close court for paint the place.'

Obieze moved his stout body from one angle to another as he sought a more comfortable position before he continued with the attack. 'And you think D.C. talk true word?'

'Ah, Chief, D.C. talk true word,' Anako replied with conviction.

Obieze moved to another line of questioning. 'Some people way go for court for this morning-time tell me say Mr MacIntosh no be for there, say another man come for tell all the people way get business for court make them go home. That be true?' Obieze asked mischievously as he well knew the answer.

'That be true,' Anako replied patiently.

'Who be the man?' Obieze asked, slyly blinking his eyes.

'Mr Jenkin,' Anako told him truthfully.

Obieze pretended that the messenger he'd sent hadn't already given him the Director of Information's name. 'Jenkin, Jenkin,' he repeated, rolling the name slowly and savouring it on his tongue. 'I no know the man!' he remarked flatly.

'He come from headquarter,' Anako informed him, hoping that the interview would not be too long in case he imparted to the Chief something he shouldn't.

Obieze looked at Anako through half closed eyes and

cleared his throat before he shot the next question. 'For which place headquarter say Mr MacIntosh go?'

Anako told him all he knew. 'They say he go leave, Chief Obieze.'

Obieze suppressed a smile and sucked his teeth. 'Oh, which day he go for leave?'

'I no fit say, Chief. I no see Mr MacIntosh since he go from court for last Friday.'

'And Mr Mason, him too go leave?'

'They say he go trek.'

'I see,' murmured Obieze, relaxing well back in his easy chair. 'So who lock court?' he shot out again from the blue, taking Anako by surprise.

Anako just stopped himself in time from telling him the truth. 'Mr Jenkin,' he said when he managed to control his nerves a little.

This reply made the Chief sit up. 'Eh?' he asked, his eyes red with anger. 'But I hear say court lock and everybody way get business for the place bin sit for shade before Mr. Jenkin reach court for tell them make them go home say court lock. How he go tell him that if he himself get key or lock court?'

Anako opened his mouth and shut it again. Blood drained from his head, through his entire body, and converged palpitatingly in his legs. Then the blood rushed up again from his feet, putting life back into him. He did not know which way to look. He cast his eyes to the ground as if somehow, by a miracle, a reply would be written for him on the sand, but none was there. He lifted his face and with effort his eyes met those of Obieze's. They were hard and steady. The full realisation of the immense stature of the man before whom he stood, hit him. This was the man who still made his own laws, despite the ones made by headquarters. This was the man in whose hands lay the power of who shall live and who shall die, whose property should be taken away to teach the person a lesson, or whose should be returned, after consenting, willingly of course, to part with half of it to the Chief. This was a man who had spies everywhere. Anako had long forgotten when he last cried, indeed how to cry, but tears were not far off now as he stood fidgeting there. He blinked them back and sighed. 'Chief Obieze, I tell you all I know,' was all he could say.

Obieze shook his head. 'I no think say you tell me everything, Mr Anako!' He opened his snuff container, took a good helping and inhaled a finger load. He wiped his nose with the back of his hand and sneezed. He cleared his throat to release a small fraction of snuff that had gone astray into his windpipe. 'No, Mr Anako,' he repeated, his voice a little croaky from the erring tobacco, 'you no tell me who be the white mans you talk to for middle of road when you start for reach here!' he berated him.

The fear in the court interpreter earlier was nothing compared to what he felt now. He knew now that his very life stood in the balance.

'Well?' asked Obieze after he thought he had given him sufficient time to think. But Anako stood tongue tied.

'Answer me!'

Anako swallowed, perspiration springing around his eyes. 'Chief,' he began in desperation. 'You yourself know, why you want for ask me?' In his fifteen years as court interpreter, or when he faced his foreign employers, he had never felt this small, or feared for his life this much. He wiped the sweat from around his eyes.

'I hear you right? You ask me question? Me, Obieze?' the Chief said in astonishment. 'Nobody do that kind thing before!'

Anako shook his head in vehement denial. 'No, Chief, you know say I no fit do that kind thing,' he whispered in a trembling voice.

Obieze let out his breath and relaxed in his chair. 'Good!' he said, nodding with approval. 'I glad for hear you say that!' He stopped and looked with narrowed eyes at Anako. 'I see say the people you work for spit for inside your mouth. You lie now like they lie,' he observed in a deceptively mild voice.

'I no lie, Chief, I tell you everything,' Anako pleaded.

Obieze ignored the agonising humiliation and plea on the court interpreter's face and instead shouted at him, 'You tell me only what they say make you tell me. You think say I be fool? You think because I just sit here say I no get ear?'

The interpreter stood with his head bowed, speechless with shame.

'Make you go, Mr Anako, I finish for talk to you!'

C

M.B.C.—C

Anako raised his eyes and met Obieze's. 'But I want for explain . . .' he started to say.

'What you want for explain?' Obieze sneered.

The court interpreter indeed had no more to say, he simply watched as Obieze went on assuaging his ego.

'Make you careful or you go be mark man!' he warned, waving a finger in the air. 'Make you come out from my face!' he ordered.

Anako bowed and retreated.

'Well, here we are!' Underwood said as he braked his car in the grounds of the native court. They both got out and stood looking around. Eze, who had spied them, walked over. 'You want something, sir?'

'No, we just look for see,' Underwood replied.

Eze felt it his duty to introduce himself in case Underwood had forgotten who he was. 'I be watchman, sir, and janitor.'

'I know, we bin meet long time before, and we bin pass you and driver for Ujo River for this afternoon-time.'

'Ah! That be true,' smiled Eze, pleased. 'Mr Anako no be for here,' he confided.

'Yes,' mumbled Underwood distractedly.

'He go see Chief,' Eze thought he'd better inform Underwood in case, from the way he was looking about him, he wondered where Anako had got to.

'I know that,' Underwood remarked and now seemed disinterested in Eze. The night-watchman. however, pressed on, 'Mr District Commissioner say he go give me increment.'

'Is that so?'

'I talk true word, sir. You think say you go fit tell Mr Anako? I bin tell him but I no think say he believe me.'

'Oh? Why he no think say you talk true word?' Underwood asked and looked at the night-watchman with more interest.

'That be the thing, master, I think he be jealous.' Eze spread his hands.

'I see, because he too no get increment?'

'You talk true word, sir!'

'Well it no matter because your pay come from headquarters. Mr Anako no get hand for the matter,' Underwood said to reassure him.

'Thank you, sir!' Eze shouted, jubilant.

'I think we go back now for headquarters. When Mr Anako come back make you tell him say we come for look round.'

'One small business lef, master. It go be too cold for sit under window for night-time. Mr Anako say make me for sit there for hear office phone ring.'

Underwood paused, looking at Eze who was trying to play his immediate superior against him. 'Well, if Mr Anako say make you sit under window, then make you sit there!'

Eze looked crestfallen. 'I see, sir,' he replied and began to walk away.

'Crafty old thing!' Bailey put in.

'Not half!' said Underwood as they both got back in the car.

Anako scarcely remembered leaving the Chief's presence but cycled blindly on his way back to the native court like a man in a dream. Never, he told himself, had he been so exposed and humiliated. It was not possible that all this should have happened to him. He was not only in disgrace, he was also a marked man, or nearly one. What was the difference? Another false move from him and he could be murdered anywhere and at any time, and no one but his employers would conduct a hopeless search. Should he report back his interview to headquarters, he asked himself over and over again as he rode. He wished that MacIntosh had not gone on leave but was still there to protect him. He sighed, tears streaming down his face.

All the time he was thinking, cycling and wiping his eyes, his head turned nervously left and right. Who was that man up the palm tree cutting down kernels? Should he really be cutting palm kernels at this time of day? Or was he waiting to throw the bunch on his head as he cycled past? Was he planted there by the Chief to do just that? And that man coming towards him on foot – he seemed to have darted out from nowhere. Could he have been sent to murder him? That young man with the palm wine keg – it's still a bit too hot for evening tapping. Maybe he is using the wine keg as a disguise? One blow on the head with a keg filled with palm wine was enough to write him off!

He couldn't remember how he got home, all he remembered was that he dismounted, threw his bicycle down and stumbled indoors. His wife, Agnes, nearly collided with him in their tiny living room cum dining room cum sleeping quarters for their children.

'I no see you look this way before. What happen?' she asked anxiously.

'I no look this way before because nothing like this way happen to me before. Agnes, something terrible happen!' His voice was thick and unnatural. His eyes had a queer, glazed expression.

Chapter Six

Underwood and Bailey drove into Utuka as the sun was setting. Utuka, the region's capital, was a flat town with only the tributary of the Ujo River to redeem what would have been a picturesque dullness. Traders had already deserted her huge market and housewives were busily engaged preparing the evening meal.

Underwood, clear of the town centre, swung his car left and left again. In five minutes he was driving through the residential area for government officials. He braked softly as he approached the home of the District Commissioner for Hughes had a thing about brake noise.

'D'you want me to come in with you?' Bailey asked hesitantly when the car stopped.

'Most certainly, after all we went on the exploration together!'

Before they were out of the car Hughes was already on the steps of his verandah. 'Well?' he asked as they approached him.

'We found some marks that we thought were made by a van,' Underwood told him.

'That does it then!' shouted Hughes with glee. 'My hunch was right after all!'

'George, we may still be wrong,' Underwood protested mildly.

'Wrong?' murmured Hughes, as if he had never heard the word before. 'You can't be, that's not possible.'

'But we haven't checked the roads leading to other sub-stations,' Underwood reminded him.

Hughes inclined his head in agreement and added, 'No, that would've been a waste of time because Maurice never went there, he went only to Ukana on trek. He got back last Friday evening with MacIntosh. He went back again on my instructions the day MacIntosh left, which was last Saturday, to collect some U.K. things for MacIntosh, and he travelled in his own car. I also saw him leave when he drove past here around tea-time yesterday, which was Sunday, on his way to the club. Since you left I've spoken to both the night-watchman and the driver at Ukana in person. The night-watchman heard the noise of a van in the early hours of this morning. Mark also informed me on his return from there this morning that the driver at Ukana told him that he'd not been out with the van for a fortnight. So, where could the van the man heard have come from?'

'Perhaps from a lorry driver who'd lost his way and tried to reverse,' Underwood countered.

Hughes waved a hand of disagreement in the air. 'Rubbish! How can a lorry driver reverse inside the yard? Near the gate perhaps.'

'But surely, George, any driver is free to do so you know? The place isn't off limits. It's public property.'

'I know it is, but the grounds of a law court, like those of a police station, unnerve people. I seriously doubt that any driver in his right senses would just drift in with his lorry, mammy-wagon or what have you, and begin to reverse it there. No, he'd be too afraid.'

Hughes waved Underwood to silence as the latter attempted to say something, and continued, 'So you see I'm right. Maurice must have returned to Ukana sometime, don't ask me when, after having had some refreshment at the club. But for what, you may well ask. I'll tell you! He must have forgotten my instructions to lock up the place when he went to collect MacIntosh's things last Saturday, and so thought, in the only possible way for Maurice to think, that he'd better slip out and do so before confronting me today.'

Underwood seized the slight pause while Hughes wiped

his face before starting up again, to contribute something. 'Maurice never went to the club before eight in the evening. I'm surprised he was there at tea-time.'

'Oh! I remember now!' Bailey interrupted. 'I forgot to add to what I told you this morning, sir, about Maurice's cook.'

'Yes, what about him?'

'Well, sir, when I first went there this morning, no one was there, and I reported this to you. Later, after my telephone conversation with Mr Anako, I went across again and found the cook's wife at their quarters. She told me that her husband left on his bicycle for Ukana about half-past three yesterday afternoon and that she'd not seen him since.'

'Why the devil didn't you tell me this before!' Hughes hissed at him.

'I was going to, sir, when Bill here came to tell me that I was to accompany him to Ukana. Also in the midst of the welter of telephone calls coming to Maurice's office, before you gave instructions that they were to be transferred to you, it slipped my mind.'

'It would. You're not the one to have a very retentive memory, are you, Bailey?' Hughes snarled at him.

'I'm sorry about it, sir,' he murmured.

Hughes turned away from him and faced Underwood. 'So you see, Bill, your guess is as good as mine about what took place. Maurice went to the club for his tea because his man was away.'

'It certainly looks that way,' Underwood remarked in some confusion.

'Looks what way?' Hughes asked in astonishment. 'My dear Bill, it *is* the way, I know I'm right!'

'Yes, you're quite right, George.'

'Good, I'm glad you acknowledge it, I like facts to be acknowledged.'

'What do we do now?' Underwood asked, sick of listening to his senior official.

Hughes's eye-brows shot up. 'Do? We follow the hounds!'

'I beg your pardon?'

'It's an expression, dear boy. You follow the hounds to catch the fox!'

Underwood spread his hands. 'But we've no hounds here,'

and I don't know whether there're any in the region,' he replied, feeling stupid.

Hughes, however, was not listening to him. He was instead voicing aloud his own thoughts. 'Exactly,' he shouted with a snap of his fingers. Underwood thought that Hughes looked like a man possessed.

'The tyre marks you saw today are our hounds!' continued Hughes in the same voice. 'Where they stopped we explore what lies beyond!' he finished, and turned to face Underwood and Bailey.

'I see,' Underwood replied. It was all he could say.

'Good, now you're beginning to show some intelligence!' Hughes told him. Bailey coughed to stop himself from laughing.

Underwood squirmed at this insult but Hughes did not seem to notice.

'For all we know Maurice may be in the village of Ukana and in all probability is still there transacting some business,' Underwood suggested in an attempt to salvage what was left of his self-respect.

'What business?' Hughes asked maliciously. When Underwood made no reply, Hughes remarked, 'Perhaps another mistress?' and quickly looked towards the lounge hoping that his wife hadn't heard.

Underwood pulled himself up. 'I would not know!'

Satisfied that Mrs Hughes was out of earshot, Hughes went on, 'No one knows anything here, do they?'

He is evil. He's like a snake, thought Underwood. One must be very, very careful or he will strike mercilessly. One need only see the devastating blow he levelled at MacIntosh to realise that such cruelty exists. Aloud he said, 'What would you like me to do?'

Hughes smiled with only his bottom teeth showing. 'Now you're showing some sense. Now you're speaking the words I like to hear! We'll go to Ukana and conduct an investigation, but first I want you and Mark to go there again. Just look at the tyre marks again. I want Mark to be another witness. You're to leave first thing in the morning and be back here before ten a.m. That'll leave me the rest of the day to marshal my plans.'

'All right,' agreed Underwood. Anything to get away from him, he thought.

'That's that then,' Hughes concluded and went into his house.

Underwood and Bailey watched him go. They stood there even after Hughes closed the big glass door leading into the lounge behind him. He always shuts it, thought Underwood, even when he is at home, to keep the noise out by day and the cries of the crickets out at night. I wonder what he does in his spare time. He shuddered. 'Incredible man!' he muttered and swore under his breath. 'Let's go,' he told Bailey. They got back into the car.

'I'll drop you off then go and see Mark, or telephone him about our errand in the morning.' He looked at his sweat-soaked shirt. 'I think I'll phone him up, I don't want to go calling on people in my present mood, and looking the way I do.'

'Are you coming to the club tonight?' Bailey asked.

Underwood heaved a sigh. 'I hadn't planned to. I was there last night and thought I'd give it a rest today and go into the township, but frankly my nerves and self respect are so shattered, I can't think of going anywhere tonight. Oh I don't know, on second thoughts I will! I'm not going to let that fool upset me!' he said as he swung his car into the drive of Bailey's home.

'Thanks a lot!' the junior secretary said in salute as he got out.

'Don't mention it. I hope you've more control of yourself than I have!'

Bailey smiled. 'See you at the club,' and waved.

Underwood nodded and pulled away.

The club with its group of small tables and cane chairs was half full when Underwood entered. Bailey was already seated at the bar toying with his second gin and tonic. Underwood waved greetings to those who looked up as he walked past in search of Jenkins. He had not been lucky in getting him at home when he phoned. Jenkins's steward had informed him that the master and his wife were at the club.

'See you later,' he called out to Bailey and made for where Jenkins and his wife, Olive, sat.

'Pretty as usual, Olive,' he said, and bowed greetings to Jenkins.

'You liar, you know you don't mean it!' she said, secretly pleased.

'In that black and white polka dot dress, with your tan and dark hair, you look a million.'

'Thank you, I think you really mean it this time. Mark said so before we left home.'

'So you see, I'm not wrong then. Mark has exquisite taste, like me!'

Olive Jenkins, who enjoyed mild flirtations now and then, slapped Underwood's thigh mildly. 'You men stick together!'

'We most certainly do!' Underwood replied in the same vein, and turned to her husband, 'Mark, you and I, like little boys, have an errand to run tomorrow.'

'Oh no! Not again!' Mrs Jenkins remarked.

'Where to now?' Jenkins put down his glass of whisky to inquire.

'To a place called Ukana.'

'Dear Lord!' cried Jenkins, 'but I've been to the wretched place only this morning!' He beckoned to a passing steward.

'I know, so have I, or to be more exact, so did we. Bailey and I got back less than hour ago. Whisky and soda please,' he told the steward hovering over their table.

'Big or small, master?'

'Big.'

The steward padded off.

'So, why have we got to go back again?' Jenkins asked with a frown.

'Bailey and I found some tyre marks. Evidently George isn't satisfied that only two pairs of eyes saw the marks, so he wants your wise old eyes to take them in. A third witness, if I may use the term more correctly.'

The steward returned with the whisky and soda. Underwood gulped half of it down.

'What time do we start in search of the Holy Grail?' Jenkins asked half mockingly.

'George didn't say what time, he just said early, but he said to get back by ten tomorrow morning.'

'Who the hell does he think he is!' shouted Jenkins.

'Lower your voice, dear,' Mrs Jenkins told him, looking about her frantically.

'No, Olive, I'm damned if I will!'

Underwood laughed and lit a cigarette. Mr and Mrs Jenkins were non-smokers. 'Well, I've delivered the message,' he said through a cloud of smoke. 'I suggest we start early, Mark, as he said, say seven.'

'Eh, give me a chance! I'm not like you, I'm a married man you know! In this climate seven in the morning's the best time to cuddle the wife and engage in the what not! But you wouldn't know that. You do yours in the township. One of these days, Bill, they'll arrest you and slap a forgery charge on you!'

Underwood who was about to have another sip from his whisky, put his tumbler down, as he was shaking with laughter. He gasped and wiped his eyes. When he gained control of himself he said, 'It takes an hour each way to Ukana, we'll allow one hour for looking at the marks. It won't be difficult, it isn't as if we'll be starting from scratch, Bailey and I have already done that.'

Chapter Seven

The coal field in Utuka region stood on the outskirts of Amaku. Every morning before the sun rose the air echoed with the ring of bicycle bells as the miners cycled to work. And each evening, as the sun set beyond the horizon, the atmosphere was subdued with the closeness of nature, and the same echo of bells accompanied the miners as they rode home tired.

Today was different, for the whole mine was shut by the authorities. The death of a miner, which the *Observer* reported to be not the usual accidental death that frequently occurred in mines, but a blatant and preconceived slaughter, had shaken everyone, including some of the miners themselves.

The *Observer*, in a scintillating editorial, had reiterated what it had been saying for months:

'UNKNOWN TO THE AUTHORITIES THE MINE IS RUN BY A HANDFUL OF MEN IN THE SECRET SOCIETY. MINERS OUT-

SIDE THIS SOCIETY ARE FACED WITH THREATS AND STRAN-
GULATION THEY ARE ALSO DENIED INCREASED WAGES AND
PROMOTION.'

The public, which had listened and supported the *Observer*
in every issue the paper championed, turned a deaf ear to
this, for surely, they argued, men who worked and breathed
as a team could not be involved in plans to deny each other
promotion and increased wages? They also felt that the
miners were too tired at the end of the day for anything
other than dinner and rest.

On the day the story was carried, Michael Adiabua, the
highly intelligent and handsome editor of the *Observer*,
summoned his news editor, Martin Ofodile, into his office
to avoid the commotion in the news room where reporters
flew in and out.

On the newspaper premises itself was a queue of people
nearly a mile long, with their heads covered with knotted
handkerchiefs, or fore-and-off caps of folded old newspapers, waiting in the heat of the day to buy copies.

Adiabua spread the day's paper before him as he and
Ofodile argued out what line to take for the follow-up
story.

'Look, Martin, I'm inclined to hold back a little now,
we've done all we can for the moment. We should let the
police take over, they're already investigating the matter.
We should sit back now and get information from them.'

But the news editor was adamant. 'We've not offended
anyone except members of the secret society. We can't be
held in contempt of court because the matter hasn't reached
the court, and the police haven't made any arrests either.
And as for sitting back to glean what information we can
from the police, we'll sit until doomsday!'

'I agree with you,' Adiabua said thoughtfully. 'I'm just
afraid that if no arrests are made, we might be asked, since
we've stated that the murder was committed by members
of the secret society in the mine, to name them.'

'Then we'll do so.'

Adiabua looked up from the paper. 'You mean you have
the names of those involved in this murder?' he asked with
surprise.

'If they're involved in this, I wouldn't know, but I know

some of them who hold responsible posts in the mine. I also gave you their names, Michael. One of the chiefs is a member. Which one, we don't know yet.'

'I know, but where do we go from there in this particular case? Knowing the names of those in the secret society is one thing, knowing the names of those involved in the murder is another.'

Ofodile wiped his spectacles and moved his short stature nearer the editor's desk. 'All right, Michael, we could start by giving the police the names of the six men, if they asked for them, who we know to be members of the society in the mine, and let them work from there.' He shook his head in despair and went on, 'I needn't tell you that the police have been unco-operative, particularly with me in the past. And much as I'd like to see them run about and sweat it out, I also realise that this is murder we're confronted with ; that we ourselves are deeply concerned. So I'll co-operate with them, but first of all I want to make one point clear and this is, whether they think that we've taken the law into our own hands, or are stepping on their toes, is beside the point as far as this incident is concerned. You'll agree with me that sometimes even the simple task of catching a thief for breaking in, is quite beyond their ability. One thing, Michael, over-rides all other issues, and that is that we'd be failing disastrously in our duty if we left this entirely to the police! There's no need to point out that our paper is the conscience and watch dog of the public – the public that cares, not the handful who'd dearly love to see us go out of publication to-morrow. We'll be remembered, if by nothing else, by this single story and, I may add, with gratitude, even if we eventually go out of print, but heaven forbid that we should. It all boils down to this, Michael. We can't soft pedal now, neither should we wait for the police to be our guide. We'll "make" the police, we shouldn't let them "make" us.'

The editor sat motionless. He took a deep breath. 'I follow the points you've made and I'm entirely in accord with them.' He looked up at his news editor who'd been standing, and smiled. 'Please sit down, Martin, and don't look so fierce – you're not airing your anger on a member of the police force! A point has just occurred to me, however,' Adiabua said as his news editor drew up a chair nearer the desk. 'And before I make this point, Martin, I want you to remember that we're trying to turn over, argue out, discard, or look for something fresh as regards this matter.' He smiled and Ofodile smiled back. 'What worries me is this. What if, after we've given the police the names of the six miners, they fail to follow it up? Dashes as you and I know, in fact as the entire public knows, exist in the force. Money in the right places could easily squash the whole thing. If that happens, with the result that this matter is blanketed over, we'll never be trusted or believed again!' He paused to make sure that his news editor grasped the full impact of what he'd said. 'And not only that,' went on Adiabua, 'we'll be left carrying the can!'

Ofodile sighed. 'The fact that bribery exists in the force shouldn't tie our hands behind our backs. On the contrary, and as you've pointed out, the knowledge that they know that we know, should make them want to do their best in this instance, I should think. And by the way, my source of information is impeccable – he's a non-society member, and was himself a miner for some years.'

'A disgruntled miner perhaps who's never been promoted, or had his pay packet reviewed?' Adiabua asked wickedly. But Ofodile missed the mockery that was intended as he replied spiritedly, 'Rubbish, Michael, this is so unlike you! My informer is no other than Daniel Okoro, our chief news vendor. You're not quite with me, Michael, are you?' He eyed Adiabua, who said softly, 'On the contrary I'm with you as I've always been. If I weren't I wouldn't have let the story get into the paper in the first place. I hate to have to say this, but Martin, you must remember that I'm the editor, therefore the one who'll be summoned to court, and even jailed, should our facts be incorrect. But that's a minor detail,' he said waving the point aside. 'Mainly, Martin, I'm concerned on your behalf as any editor should be. At the same time I'm also thinking of the future of the paper as a whole. If we slip up with this one, the reputable standing the paper and we enjoy, will be wiped out overnight! I don't doubt you as you seem to think. We've worked together for many years, and you should know that by now, but this story is different from any we've handled all the years we've known each other, or are ever likely to handle again. Martin, believe me, I just want to be quite sure.'

Ofodile replied through tight lips. 'A man died not from being trapped inside the coal face, nor did he drown in the pit. He was found dead at the pit head, with his throat cut, I'll stand or fall by this!'

Adiabua looked at him steadily. 'Right! What else have you got on the story?'

Ofodile relaxed. 'I heard from Daniel that the council of elders broke up this afternoon when we threw a free copy of the paper I gave him in to them, as I'd instructed.'

Adiabua looked at him with surprise. 'A free paper? My friend we can't afford to hand out free copies, our circulation is only six thousand in a region of one million people.'

'I know what I'm doing. Believe me. I wouldn't have done it were it not for the fact that my informer told me that all those elders are members of the secret society.'

'But surely, giving them a free paper when they're all very wealthy . . .'

Ofodile sighed inwardly. Michael must have got out on the wrong side of the bed this morning. But he told him, 'I agree they are wealthy but the action was meant to jolt them, in case they thought no one knew how the man died. And when the full story comes out, together with the court proceedings, it'll help to kick them all out of office.'

'Martin, please! One battle at a time!' cried Adiabua.

Ofodile ignored the cry and went on, 'The secrets of the society would then be bared for all to see, and they will not lift their heads up again. I tell you, Michael, those men are holding the region down. We should get rid of them. Only when we do that, shall we be able to clean up the mine.'

'I see,' replied Adiabua, deep in thought. 'But you don't intend to show your hand too much until arrests are made, do you?'

Ofodile smiled at his editor's anxiety. 'No, but I thought we'd build up the heat, indirectly of course, until it nearly chokes them. Then, when they can bear it no longer, they'll start trickling in one by one to the office, either to threaten us to lay off, or bear the consequences, or deny that they are involved. It's often surprising what fear, plus a guilty conscience, makes one do. The victim often becomes irrational and loses grip of his senses. We'll see just how strong they are when exposed.'

Adiabua shook his head at the uncompromising Ofodile.

'D'you have the editorial for tomorrow's paper with you?'

'Yes, and it's going on the front page.' He then added hastily, 'If it's all right with you.'

'Of course.'

Ofodile handed the editorial across. Adiabua read it and stared at it for some minutes. 'I'm not sure about the last line.'

Ofodile strained forward to see what he had written at the end that his editor did not like. 'You mean what I said about those of us with a conscience, as well as the paper, should act as vigilantes . . .'

'Yes, it sounds very much like *Onward Christian Soldiers*!'

'But that's what we are!'

Adiabua agreed wearily. 'In a way, yes, but that line can be deleted and the rest of the editorial will still convey our stand. Let's not also involve the public. I don't like to be at the head of something that reads as if I'm marching a group into Zion!'

'All right,' Ofodile said, giving way a little, 'I'll take the offending line out. By the way, Godfrey rang from Ukana to say that the District Officer is missing.'

Adiabua who had been sitting sideways, swivelled round with a gasp. 'What?'

'Just that,' said Ofodile, folding up the copy of the editorial. 'He also asked whether you or I would ring Utuka to get them to confirm it. I gather he prised the story out of the government's old night-watchman at Ukana.'

'Why can't he ask the Commissioner about it himself? He's near there?'

Ofodile scratched his forehead. 'Yes, well, he said it'd carry more weight if you phoned him, and he is right.'

'But how could a D.O. be missing, for goodness' sake?'

'Godfrey couldn't tell me that either. Actually he has a good reason for not wanting to approach the Commissioner, and prefers it to be done by remote control. The D.O. was only missed this morning and only a handful of people know or suspect it, and his source of information is among the latter. It'd put the man in jeopardy. Godfrey, only this morning, made the contact with a pound as bait. Anyway, he fears for the night-watchman if he goes straight back to the Commissioner and begins to ask questions.'

Adiabua looked at his watch, it said half past five. No use phoning now as none of the officials would be available, he thought. 'I'll give the D.C. a ring in the morning. By the way, how are the mechanics getting on with the machine? Nasty business for it to break down early this morning. As if we haven't enough on our hands without that happening!'

'I gather from the circulation manager that it didn't affect the print run or our sales.'

'That's something to be thankful for, I suppose.'

'Well,' Ofodile said, getting up, 'I'd better go and finish up with the rest of the items for the paper.'

Adiabua picked up the receiver after his news editor had left. 'The works manager please.'

Seconds later a voice came through. 'Aguilo here.'

'Aguilo, how's it going?'

'Not too bad not too good. We're a bit behind as you know due to the paper being late out today. The front page is ready minus the editorial, which I gather will go there. Then we'll strike the proof. By the way, sir, two of our typographical machines aren't working.'

'I'll be down in . . .' Adiabua began and stopped as Ofodile burst into the office.

'Michael! Oh, I'm sorry. I had no idea you were on the phone. I'll come back later.'

Adiabua covered the mouth of the receiver. 'No, what's the matter?'

'News has just come in that a miner has hanged himself in his home!'

'What? When?'

'Details are still coming in.'

Adiabua removed his hand from the mouth of the receiver. 'Look, Aguilo, I'll call you back!' He turned to Ofodile. 'I'll come with you. What's the dead man's name?' he asked, as they walked out of his office together.

'Agba. Josiah Agba.'

'What made him hang himself I wonder?'

'We don't know yet.'

'When did it happen?'

'This afternoon. I gather that after he'd had breakfast he

went back to lie down to have more rest as the mine isn't operating today. His wife didn't disturb him until lunch was nearly ready. When she went to wake him she found him hanging from their bedroom ceiling. She ran out screaming and some of the other tenants who were with her, also ran out. They're furious, of course, as they won't be able to go near or touch their possessions in the house for a year when the hanging is remedied with ceremonial rights. One of them was bathing when she heard the screams, and ran out clutching her loin cloth. The only item of clothing she has in the world now for a whole year!'

'You've a reporter covering the story of course?'

'Yes, the same one who broke the news.'

Adiabua nodded with satisfaction. 'We'll use it as the lead story. The follow-up story on the mine murder, we'll use as the second lead. I'm going down to see the works manager, two of our machines are out of order. Send the copy down as soon as it's ready. We'll manage somehow, but don't ask me how!'

The two stopped at the door of the news room watching four out of their eight reporters at work. 'I think the best thing to do,' the editor continued, 'is to send out two of those chaps to interview all the tenants where the hanging took place. Get their reactions on how the hanging will affect their lives. Tell the photographer to go along with them. We'll fill up all the pages of tomorrow's paper with the murder and the hanging stories. Whatever room that's left, and I doubt if there'll be any, we'll fill in with the pictures taken at the inter-tribal football match. Keep every member of the editorial staff in, except the reporters who are out covering the story. The messengers as well. Tell that telephone girl who's always itching to go home, that she's to stay or risk being fired! One more thing, ring Godfrey and tell him to come up first thing in the morning. He'll be more useful here at the moment than at Utuka or Ukana, whichever one he's in at present.'

Adiabua and Ofodile parted. Adiabua ran his eyes round the works looking for the manager. He found him behind one of the two machines that were at fault. 'Mr Aguilo!' he shouted. Work stopped, no one had seen him enter and all eyes turned towards him. 'Tell that man there to stop mounting the pages, we're starting all over again!' he ordered.

Aguilo, with two faulty machines on his hands, cried out in anguish, 'What did you say?'

Three men stood on a street corner in deep and breathless conversation. To Daniel Okoro, the chief news vendor who watched unobserved, the men made an interesting study in repose.

Daniel Okoro, once a miner turned chief news vendor, worked as an informer and errand boy to the news editor. He had an axe to grind in the murder case as he had relinquished his job as a miner to escape the tyranny of the secret society. When he joined the *Observer*, he used his expert knowledge in team work to organise the vendors under him. He never married as he felt that he could not maintain a family on a miner's pay. Even when he became a vendor and earned more money, he still remained single, preferring the company of his men friends by day, which enabled him to hear all that went on in the township. At night, however, he preferred his mistress. He therefore enjoyed the best of both worlds. His mistress never visited his home, rather it was he who went to hers. Each morning before the town was astir, she saw him off as he left to collect, distribute and go on his own paper rounds.

Daniel sat on the verandah of his home between sunset and the start of darkness, wearing only a singlet and loin cloth as it was so hot. It was too early yet for him to call on his mistress, the lovely Evangelina. As she would not have finished cooking his evening meal, he thought he would kill time by airing himself and at the same time watch people going by.

What fascinated Daniel Okoro about the men he was watching was their highly agitated lips, which suggested to him that it was no ordinary conversation they were holding. Coupled with this fact was the suspicion that somewhere, sometime, he had seen some of those men before. Daniel Okoro tried lip reading but it proved unsuccessful, so he gave that up and sat back to watch them.

He watched until the three men finished their conversation and parted. He sighed then left the verandah to go and get ready for his visit to Evangelina.

Michael Adiabua, the editor of *The Daily Observer*, and

Martin Ofodile, his news editor, stood in the works department watching the pages being mounted. 'Well, the stories have certainly filled up all eight pages,' Adiabua said with satisfaction.

Ofodile looked at his watch. It said eight-fifteen. 'We've managed quite well despite the fact that we were handicapped by two broken-down machines. I think you should complain to the management about these you know. They're all antiquated. The printing machine should've been written off ages ago.'

Adiabua nodded his agreement, but went on to enlighten his news editor. 'Lack of funds, they'll say. I've told them about the machines on several occasions. I've warned them that one day the paper won't come out at all. After each warning they all say the same thing – lack of funds; the paper is not making enough money to justify buying a new printing machine. So, where do we go from there?'

'Nowhere at all, except that it's such an awful pity.'

'I agree whole-heartedly.'

They stood, thoughtful, for some seconds. It was Ofodile who broke the silence. 'D'you think we'll put the paper to bed before midnight?' he asked, looking at his wrist watch again.

'I wouldn't like to hazard a guess,' Adiabua told him as he rubbed his eyes wearily. 'Our only saving grace is that this is the only newspaper in the region, and like it or not, the people must wait for it, however late it comes out.'

'By the way, Michael, is there any truth in the story that some of our noted and wealthy detractors are hatching a plot to set up a rival newspaper?'

'I've heard the story too. I very much doubt that it'll come to anything though, they'd run into difficulties. Whereas we're entirely independent and our hands are clean, their paper would serve as a mouthpiece for their secret ambitions – financial and political, though mainly political, I should think. Anyway, I wouldn't worry about that if I were you. By the time theirs, or any other newspaper, appears on the scene, we'll be too well established for petty rivalry.'

'If only we had up to date machines,' Ofodile lamented.

'Yes,' Adiabua sighed. 'The printing press as you well know is held together with fisherman's rope. Four of our typographical machines over there are held in place with hairpins. Ink sometimes spludges all over the paper as it's being printed, and you can't see what you're reading half of the time. The paper we print on is bad quality. Sometimes I wonder what the fuss is all about, why people spend their hard-earned pennies to buy it? Why they bother to read it at all!'

'As you've said, we're the only paper.'

'Only by the grace of God, otherwise we'd all be out looking for new jobs!' Adiabua pointed out, and turned to the works manager. 'Mr Aguilo, there's nothing more for me to do here, I'll be in my office if you want me.' He walked out of the dusty newspaper premises with his news editor. Halfway to the office building they stopped. 'So we have all that's to be had on the story?' he asked Ofodile again.

'For the moment, yes.'

'The more I think of the murder, the more it shatters me. It's an incredible thing to happen. What could be the real reason behind it, I wonder!'

'I don't know, Michael, but we'll find out in due course, as the story unfolds.'

Adiabua glanced up at the office building and saw some members of the staff milling about on the balcony. 'You can tell some of those fellows to go home. Keep back a reporter or two just in case,' he told Ofodile, and added, 'If this story is going to run for some time, and I suspect it will, we must rotate the staff working hours, which lot goes home early, and on what days, and vice versa.'

'I'll see to that.'

'In the meantime let's keep our fingers crossed and hope the police are doing their uttermost. It's all right to act as the people's watchdog and as the instrument that revives their conscience, but what we don't want the paper to be is the judge, the jury and the hangman as well!'

'I follow your point,' said Ofodile with respect and a smile.

Adiabua patted him on the back. 'Good,' he said, and then went on after a pause, 'By the way, Martin, you said something earlier about one of the chiefs being a member of the secret society. Any chance of our knowing which one?'

'None. People are always scared about giving that sort of

information. No one wants to be the fellow who gave his chief away as his life, and those of his family, would be made very miserable in the village if it came out later. And I doubt whether even Daniel knows. It's awfully difficult, Michael.'

'I see.'

Chapter Eight

Jenkins raced from the bedroom and down the stairs in his haste. 'I'm coming,' he shouted as the continuous banging on his front door went on. When he opened it to Underwood he said acidly, 'There are several ways of routing people out of their homes at an ungodly hour, and I'm not sure that I like yours.'

'You tell me the others and I'll try them out!' he replied jovially.

'You can start by ringing the door bell, for instance – there is a door bell you know, on the left hand side, see?' said Jenkins, pressing the bell.

Underwood grinned. 'I did that but no one answered.'

'Hmm,' mumbled Jenkins, shrugging his arms into a light-coloured linen jacket.

'You won't need that, you'll be roasted by the time we're back,' Underwood told him.

'Olive insisted. She likes to see me immaculately dressed. I've no option but to follow her bidding. I'm not like you with no one standing at your elbow to nag you,' Jenkins reminded him quietly, buttoning up his jacket.

'I'm not too sure, I wish I had Olive to nag me sometimes,' Underwood teased.

'Not on your nelly, she's mine alone, not like Johnson's wife who every man except me wants!' Jenkins said as he got into the car.

'Now that you mentioned them, where are they? They weren't at the club last night,' Underwood turned to say.

'Why ask me? I don't know where they are. Arthur's

becoming too skittish for my nerves. You can't offer his wife a drink without his imagining you've an ulterior motive!'

'Yet he wasn't always like that,' observed Underwood.

'She's too young for him if you ask me, and the age difference is beginning to wear him out. You can't do at forty-eight what you did at twenty, the heart pumps a bit faster! And he's worried that someone may do it faster than he, with his wife!'

'Twenty-two years is rather a big difference,' said Underwood as he steered out of the government premises.

'I agree,' shouted Jenkins, blinking his eyes against the headlights of an oncoming lorry. 'I look at Olive and thank my stars. She's only a couple of years younger than my forty-six years.'

'I wonder how and where they met, the Johnsons I mean,' Underwood went on.

'In Las Palmas I gather. She sailed in from Lisbon to continue her holiday, and he sailed in from the coast on his way home on leave. He left the boat at Las Palmas, deciding to wait for another mail-boat which would give him a few days there. They met in the foyer of an hotel, through mutual friends. Don't ask me who the friends were because I don't know. However, to cut a long story short, they fell in love, got married, and she came out with him.'

'Beautiful girl.'

'Yes indeed, and you should see her with her clothes off! I often catch a glimpse of her sunbathing on their balcony. She's going through a bad patch with Arthur, I gather from Olive.'

'But I always thought Arthur to be gregarious.'

'He was, and for that matter, still is, when the mood takes him! Particularly when he's not with his wife.'

'Pity they should turn sour on each other,' commented Underwood as he changed gear.

'D'you fancy her in bed?'

'Who doesn't?'

'I don't!'

'Ah, that's because you have Olive, and you're both still in love with each other.'

'Why don't you try matrimony sometime, Bill? It's very rewarding you know,' said Jenkins looking at him.

'And very distracting too, if you're honest. No, for the moment I'll continue to sow my wild oats!'

'No matter where they sprout?'

'That's the best part!' Underwood laughed.

'You're nauseating!'

'Thank you.'

Jenkins involuntarily raised his right leg. 'Careful, there's a goat in front of you!'

Underwood swerved and straightened up. 'If I'd hit him. we'd have thrown it in the boot and carried it home – it's good meat!'

'No thank you, I prefer to have mine inspected first!'

'You're spoilt, Mark. Olive spoils you!'

'As I said, I'm not the one to quibble about the serenity of my home life,' Jenkins remarked as he settled back more comfortably to enjoy the morning drive.

'Well here we are – Ukana at last. Eight o'clock, bang on time.'

Jenkins sat up and looked about him. 'Do we get out here and start hiking?' he asked with a yawn.

'No, we drive into the road leading into the township. Bailey and I marked the important parts.'

'Thank heavens for that. So all we need do really is just coast along until we hit the places?'

'Yes, and you cast your tired and trusted old eyes towards it, and report back to George when we get back that you've seen what Bailey and I said we saw.'

'I see, well drive on, Murdoch, drive on!'

'I like that. I thought it was Horatio!'

'I invent my characters!'

They drove past the half-mile sign on the main thorough-fare and branched off on the road entering the township. Half-way down it Underwood glanced about for any sign of the stones that they had placed on various parts as reminders, but he saw nothing.

'Funny,' remarked Underwood, speaking more to himself than to his companion. 'I can't see the stones. We placed them in three places and not as far down the road as this. They all seem to have vanished.'

'So what do we do now?' Jenkins asked as he caught Underwood's last sentence.

'Do? I don't know yet. Let's drive back again. We'll re-

verse over there, by that tree,' he pointed with his chin.
'Maybe I was going too fast and missed them. Anyway we'll
soon see. Mark, keep your eyes alert won't you? Particularly on the left hand side of the road.'

Underwood drove back to the beginning of the road. 'Did
you see anything?'

'Nothing, as they say in these parts.'

'It means then that we'll have to get out and leg it. We'll
do all over again what Bailey and I did yesterday afternoon,'
he said angrily.

Jenkins, who wasn't keen on that idea, asked, 'Isn't there
a shorter cut to what you've just suggested?'

Underwood shook his head. 'No, Mark. We've driven
twice now along this road and we've seen nothing. All
traces of the van's marks were completely wiped out, the
stones have also disappeared. In the circumstances, what
else d'you suggest we do?'

Jenkins took a deep breath and slowly let it out. 'I don't
frankly know. You think the wind ... ?'

'What wind?'

'Or people's feet?'

'Perhaps,' Underwood conceded, 'but it wouldn't have
completely erased them. They were heavy streaks.'

'D'you think they were deliberately removed?'

'I don't know, but who could've done it, and for what
reason?'

Jenkins spread his hands. 'Search me, I don't know. Anyway we'd better get on with it, it's nearly half-past eight
and as you've said, George wants us back at ten.'

The two performed the same task that Bailey and Underwood had the previous day, but this time without success.
Finally they decided to call it a day.

'We'll drive back to Utuka,' said Underwood, getting into
the car, in a bad mood. 'We'll call in at the native court
here on our way. I want to ask the interpreter how he's getting on.'

'That'll take up our time – we're supposed to be back
at ten.'

'Yes, I know, but it'll only take a few minutes,' replied
Underwood as he drove into the court grounds.

Eze, the night-watchman, came out at the sound of a car.

Before Underwood stopped he was already standing beside the car.

'Good morning, sir!'

'Ah, good morning,' replied Underwood. 'You be the man I bin see for inside van yesterday with driver.'

'Yes, sir,' Eze replied, pleased that Underwood still remembered their meeting at Ujo River.

'For which place be Mr Anako?' Underwood asked him.

'He no come yet. I think the reason he no come yet because court lock.'

'Make you go tell him say I want for speak with him.'

Eze trotted off.

Jenkins turned to Underwood. 'Remind me, Bill, to ask George for the duplicate keys here. It just occurred to me that the place can't be painted inside if it's locked. The outside maybe.'

'Oh yes of course. If only I'd remembered it yesterday afternoon I'd have brought the keys down with me.'

'I wonder what MacIntosh found to do here?' Jenkins wondered out loud, changing the subject.

'I suppose the affairs of Ukana kept him busy. He's the zealous type I gather. The work has grown through the years, you know.'

'Ah there you are, Mr Anako.'

'Good morning, sir, I hear say you want to speak to me.'

'That be true. I just want for know how everything be.'

'It no bad, sir,' Anako replied and hesitated. He looked undecided whether to say more or not. He decided to go on. 'I just get small palaver with Chief.' When Underwood and Jenkins looked surprised, Anako went on, 'I think I bin tell you yesterday for afternoon-time when we cross for township road say, Chief send word say, he want for see me. And headquarter tell me also say, make I go tell Chief Obieze say, Court lock.'

When the men in the car nodded to this, Anako cleared his throat and continued, 'Well, I see Chief, what he tell me make all my body shake!'

'What he tell you?' Underwood asked slowly.

Anako looked from one expatriate to the other. 'Obieze tell me say I be mark man,' he told them, emphasising each word.

'What does that mean?' Jenkins broke in on the two-sided conversation to ask.

'It mean they go watch me, and maybe put trap for me for catch me.'

Underwood and Jenkins looked at each other. 'Why he say that?' Underwood took up the conversation again.

'Well you see, sir, for yesterday when I cross you and Mr Bailey for road, you bin tell me say, make I no tell Obieze say, it be Mr Mason who lock court, say, make I just say we want for paint court.'

'So?'

'Chief Obieze say I lie, say I just tell him what head-quarter want make me for tell him.'

'What!' exclaimed Underwood and turned to look at Jenkins. 'The rascal may know as much or even more than we do! What make him say that?' he asked, now addressing Anako.

'I no know, but he get spy for every road and for every place. And they tell him say me and you talk for road before I go see him. He even know Mr Jenkin here come for here after court lock.'

'How d'you mean?' Jenkins asked, his hand trembling as he stroked his badly shaven chin.

'Well you see, sir, Chief ask me for which place Mr MacIntosh and Mr Mason go. I tell him say Mr MacIntosh go leave and Mr Mason go for trek. Then he ask me why court lock, and I tell him like Mr Underwood tell me for say, we want for paint the place. He no believe me because he tell me say nobody paint when rain go soon come. So he ask me who lock court?' Here Anako paused and looked apologeti-cally at Jenkins. 'I tell him you lock court, I no know the reason he ask, and Mr Underwood him tell me say make I no tell him it be Mr Mason. And I no bin know say Obieze know Mr Jenkin come for morning-time yesterday.'

'So?' Jenkins asked in a squeaky voice, fingering his tie.

'He ask me how you go lock court when you come to Ukana for morning-time after court lock.'

'And what did you say?' asked Jenkins, breathing very fast.

'After that, sir, I no fit say nothing.'

'Well, well, well!' exclaimed Jenkins nervously. 'The old

boy certainly has an efficient spy network! Wait until Olive hears this!' he added, but he was not amused.

'Wait here, Mr Anako. Mark, come with me for a minute,' said Underwood. They got out of the car and walked away a few yards. 'In view of this, Mark, I think it only fair to mention to the interpreter about our fruitless search for the stones.'

'But the two bear no relation, or so I'd have thought.'

'Even so,' said Underwood, scratching his head, 'he may have some ideas. We can't lose anything by telling him. On the other hand we might gain something. Besides, the poor chap's already in trouble on my account. It might help to take his mind off the Chief's threats. He's worried to death.'

'So am I, but the difference is I suppose I'm not a native and don't live here. Still, as you wish, but I think it'd be pointless, and above all else I don't think it's a wise step, not at the moment anyway.'

'Look, Mark, we need as much help as possible with this. He may've seen someone as he cycled back from the Chief's yesterday, removing those stones, and never gave it a thought that they're important, and that we placed them there ourselves purposely.'

'But this place is full of people loitering about in the streets, picking things up and putting them down again, as you well know.'

'There's no comparison. We're looking for something vital.'

'A few lost cowries or manila are also vital to them,' Jenkins pointed out.

'Bailey did tell me yesterday to mention to the interpreter about Maurice's aspect of this matter, but I thought we'd act on the D.C.'s say so. Now I'm not so sure,' said Underwood speaking more to himself.

'And I think you thought wisely yesterday. There's no point in adding fat to the fire, it'll only confuse him more.'

'All right.'

They went back to the car where Anako was standing. 'Look, Mr Anako,' said Underwood. 'Everything go be all right. We go send duplicate keys for you.'

'Thank you, sir.'

'As for Chief, make you no worry about him, we go look after you if he try for make trouble. O.K.?'

'Thank you, sir!'

'Right, we leave everything for your hand now. In the meantime make you find people for help paint court.'

'And hire new caretaker,' Jenkins put in.

'I go do that, sir.'

'D'you think it's any use combing the township road again?' Underwood inquired as they drove off.

'None whatsoever.'

'George won't like our going back empty handed.'

'What's the alternative?' Jenkins turned sideways to ask. 'Lie?' When Underwood did not reply he went on, 'Heaven forbid! I won't lie or make up a story just to please him!' Jenkins said with vehemence.

'So what do we tell him?'

'The truth of course, what else? And for all we know Maurice may've turned up at Utuka before we get there.'

'I most certainly hope so.'

Jenkins thought for a few minutes. 'Look, Bill, we've done our best, we can't fish out tyre marks where they don't exist.'

'They were there yesterday, Mark. They were obliterated, I'm certain of that.'

'So, do we go and put them back? Frankly I don't see the reason for your worry.'

'I do,' Underwood said between his teeth. 'I'm worried because George will never believe we saw those marks yesterday. He'll point out to me with glee that Bailey and I aren't to be trusted. I don't need to tell you how he enjoys gloating over other people's errors. He'll swear that he'll never again send us out on an important mission.'

'If that's all that's worrying you, I'd say that you're worrying unnecessarily. Let him find other errand boys, or better still he can jolly well run his little errands himself!'

Underwood took a hand away from the steering wheel to rub his eyes and said quietly, 'Deep marks made by a van when it braked suddenly don't vanish overnight, that's another reason for my worry.'

'You think someone covered them over?' Jenkins asked with a frown.

Underwood put the car into third gear. 'Yes.'

Jenkins thought wildly. 'Who for heaven's sake?'

'Anako has just informed us that the local Chief has spies everywhere, or have you forgotten?'

'Now look, Bill . . .'

'Now look nothing!' Underwood retorted, his nerves frayed. 'If the old boy's spies told him that Anako had a chat with Bailey and me yesterday, there's nothing to stop him from knowing that we placed stones at some strategic points on the road.'

'I see what you mean.'

'Good!'

'But what would they be doing that for?'

'Perhaps they've involved with Maurice.'

'Bill,' said Jenkins softly, as if trying to rescue someone contemplating suicide from a tall building before he jumped. 'You're going a bit far. Maybe the spies, and I'm following your train of thought, removed the stones and covered up the tyre marks out of pique.'

'Why? Tell me why they should do that and I'll believe you.'

'Perhaps a sort of tit for tat, since our man annoyed the Chief.'

Underwood considered this. 'Hmm, perhaps, or possibly to hide something?'

'In this day and age? In 1935? With us here? Bill, use your head!' Jenkins exclaimed.

'The world may be old, Mark, but our habits are still very young. Here they're even younger,' Underwood observed quietly.

Jenkins looked at him with his mouth open. They drove the rest of the way to Utuka without exchanging another word.

On reaching the government offices they braked and got out. 'We're going straight to see George,' said Underwood unnecessarily, walking ahead.

Jenkins, himself a tall man, increased his stride to catch up with him. They knocked and entered the imposing office of the District Commissioner. Hughes looked up. 'Well?'

'It was no good,' Underwood told him.

'What?' Hughes asked, numbed. He looked hard at Underwood. 'But it was only yesterday that you told me the operation was a success.'

Underwood sighed. 'Yes, I know, but it has now proved a failure. I'm sorry, sir.'

'How could it be? How could something you seemed certain about yesterday take a different turn overnight? I'm afraid I don't understand. Doubtless with some explanation I may be able to understand it,' Hughes said, stunned.

'It also bothers me, I don't understand it either,' Underwood said, defensively.

'What d'you think happened, Mark?' Hughes asked the Director of Information who, hitherto, had played the part of an innocent bystander.

'I don't know. Since I didn't see the marks yesterday, I don't really know what to say.'

Hughes reverted back to Underwood. 'You're certain that those marks were there yesterday?'

'I am, and I'll swear to it. We can, if you doubt me, call Bailey in to verify it,' Underwood said belligerently.

Hughes dismissed the mention of Bailey with a flick of his hand. 'He's no good, I'd have been much happier and more confident if Mark here could've seconded your story. As it is, I'm not so sure now.'

Underwood saw red. 'You mean you didn't believe me yesterday? You think we cooked up the whole story?'

Hughes looked at him, slightly amused. 'I didn't say that.'

'But you implied it!' Underwood pointed out frostily.

Hughes's full attention was arrested. He could not quite believe his ears that he was being so harshly addressed. 'My dear fellow, I've only one objective and whose feelings I trample on to reach that end doesn't come into it at all! I have one sole purpose, and that is to get Maurice back. He's still not back and hasn't been in touch with us either. If you're going to nurse what may appear to you a wounded ego, by all means go ahead. I have a one track mind on this issue. Your feeling of wounded pride will be nothing compared with what I'll feel later when the Governor lashes out at me!' he shouted.

This outburst subdued Underwood for a second, then he went on again, doggedly, 'I don't know whether this information will be of any use to you now, in view of the low opinion you have of my ability . . .'

Hughes cut him short. 'I tell you it wasn't meant that way!'

'Anyway,' continued Underwood, 'our man, the court interpreter at Ukana, told us that the Chief set his spies on him yesterday, and for that matter, may have done so on us.'

'Oh?' replied Hughes and gestured for further enlightenment which precipitated Underwood to continue, this time in a much more friendly tone. 'I gather the Chief knew about Mr Anako stopping to have a word with Bailey and myself yesterday before the interpreter even reached his presence to answer a summons from him, and also to deliver our message.'

'Oh? That's interesting,' said Hughes, his hazel eyes steady.

'He must surround himself with a great deal of people who do nothing but tell him what's going on,' observed Underwood, life coming back into him.

Hughes sighed. 'That's nothing. So do we except we call ours contact men, and we haven't as many, I shouldn't think, as the Chief. But please go ahead and tell me what you're thinking.'

'Well, as I've already told Mark, if the Chief knew about our movements yesterday, there's nothing to stop his henchmen from being aware of, and indeed moving the stones we left. Mark, here, suggested that they may have done so out of pique as our man, I gather, told the Chief a lie about Mark locking the court.'

'Now you have me, I'm completely at sea,' said Hughes, but he still looked intently at Underwood.

'I told Anako not to tell the Chief that Maurice locked the court.'

'Why in heaven's name did you do that?'

'I felt that the least known about the matter by others besides ourselves, the better.'

'I see,' Hughes replied and sighed again.

Jenkins cleared his throat. 'If I may say something here, George, I think the driver's as well as the court messengers's wives should be told. They're not what we might call in this instance outsiders. They're directly involved. I'm wholly in agreement with what Bill says, but the line should be drawn after the five women, and not before.'

'Why should it?' Hughes asked annoyed.

Jenkins swallowed back what he was about to say. 'It was just an idea . . .'

'But surely, they're used to their husbands being away for a few days? I don't see why this should be any different.'

'I'm aware of that, but the circumstances in this case are different,' Jenkins pointed out.

Hughes doodled with his pen. 'I see what you mean,' he said sourly, 'but I don't think we should tell them yet; not until all the facts are in anyway,' he added thoughtfully, and went on to something else. 'I received a stupid phone call from the editor of the *Observer*.'

Jenkins's eyebrows shot up. 'Oh?'

Seeing the look of surprise on Jenkins's face, Hughes continued, 'The clot wanted to know, in fact told me, that he'd gathered from a very reliable source, that I'd lost my District Officer and wanted me to verify it.' He stopped and looked at Jenkins inquiringly.

The Director of Information took a nervous step forward. 'If you think I told him . . .'

Hughes waved at him to keep quiet. 'I don't for one moment think you did. However I asked him to tell me where he got the story from, and d'you know what he said? I'll try and use his exact words, "It's you who should be giving me news!" He's insufferable, his arrogance is quite beyond me – the little so and so.'

Jenkins and Underwood exchanged glances and suppressed their smiles at the thought that Hughes had at last met his match!

Jenkins broke the short silence. 'But don't you think, George that if we took him into our confidence he might be able to help us? He's a very reasonable man, I've met him.'

Hughes shook his head. 'I've heard all that bosh about not fighting the press, but making friends with them instead. If I were to in this instance, it'd have terrible repercussions. If it got out that a District Officer was missing, there would be nothing stopping any of us here from being missing. We may find ourselves lifted out, singly or *en masse* in our bed clothes, unwillingly one night, and after the initial wave of shock had worn off, we'd be listed as missing persons. No expatriate would be safe any longer if this story got out! I may be earning my meal ticket here, but I'll be damned if I'll sign my death warrant as well!'

'I wonder how they got on to the story?' Jenkins puzzled out loud.

'That reporter that called here yesterday . . . d'you suppose he found out anything?' Hughes asked.

'Godfrey? If he did it wasn't from me,' said Jenkins defensively.

Hughes held his head and moaned. 'Look, Mark, will you please stop behaving as if you're under fire! No one has accused you of anything!'

'D'you think Bailey inadvertently let it out?' Underwood asked. 'Don't forget that he was handling the matter before Mark and I came into it.'

'He had specific instructions while I was in here with you yesterday, to say nothing on the subject to the reporter,' Jenkins reminded Hughes.

'Under pressure perhaps?' Hughes queried. 'Godfrey, or whatever he's called, is very agile and quick thinking I've found. He button-holed me one day and I had to be very rude to get away from him.'

'Yes, he's pretty astute,' Jenkins conceded. 'He came up to Ukana yesterday directly after I got there.'

Hughes looked at him quickly. 'Oh? What axe did he have to grind there?'

'Just nosing around, as he put it. Besides, George, he is a reporter you know. He's free to come and go anywhere he thinks there's news,' Jenkins said heavily.

'But don't you think it odd that he followed you up? He may've put two and two together.'

Jenkins said as patiently as he could, 'He may have done, but I doubt it. I also warned our staff there to say nothing to him.' He didn't add, however, that Onyeso caught him with an armful of confidential papers on the window ledge. The less said about that, the better, he thought.

Hughes sighed and wiped the perspiration from his face. 'You'd have thought that the mine murder was enough to keep the whole of them busy, but no, they have to poke their noses into this as well! By the way, have you seen today's paper?' he asked them, picking it up.

'No, we've not had a chance to, or for breakfast for that matter," Underwood informed him.

Hughes did not seem to be listening. 'I see there's been a hanging,' he told his audience quietly.

'I didn't know Everette went up on a job,' said Jenkins, craning towards the paper.

Everette Miles was the expatriate hangman, a stockily built man with muscles to match, who drowned himself with whisky after every job. He and his wife Joan made an interesting couple. Whereas Everette was rough and muscular, Joan Miles was slim and affectedly cultured. One suspected that she tried hard to brush off her husband's job as something she did not approve of, but that Miles, as every man should, had to do something, even if that something was hanging. 'We all have to contribute in Empire building,' was her favourite phrase.

'No, this didn't involve Everette,' Hughes was now saying. 'The man in the paper hanged himself at lunchtime yesterday. I haven't read the whole story yet.'

'Well, at least that's one man that's given Everette a breathing space. He won't have that on his conscience!' Underwood remarked jokingly.

'Hmm. I could never have him in the house for anything more than cocktails. I could never look at Everette without seeing hanging written all over him,' said Hughes.

'We all of us have to make a living,' observed Jenkins, feeling a little sorry for the man they were castigating.

Hughes put the paper aside saying, 'I suppose so. Look, I'm inclined to go along with Bill. I want you, Bill, to send a message to Chief Obieze telling him that I'd like to see him here at his earliest convenience.'

Chapter Nine

'Not a bad paper considering that at midnight we weren't even sure that we'd come out at all,' said the editor leafing through the pages.

'No, not bad at all,' agreed his news editor, Ofodile.

'By the way, did you get in touch with Godfrey?'

'Yes, he said he'll be down this afternoon.'

'Good, let me know when he arrives.' As an afterthought Adiabua asked, 'How's the paper selling?'

'Every copy's sold.'

'Pity we can't have a reprint run,' sighed Adiabua.

'The machine won't stand up to it.'

'No, I know. What have you in mind for tomorrow's paper?'

'I thought we might pursue the same story. I gather the police have been to the tenement house.'

'Send a reporter down to the police station . . .'

'I've already done so,' Ofodile told the editor.

'Is he back yet?'

'He wasn't five minutes ago.'

'Bring the layout for tomorrow's paper to my office when it's ready,' said Adiabua.

'I wan't for see Chief.'

'What you want?'

'I get message for him from headquarter.'

'What message say?'

'Me no know. I get message for inside paper,' said Christopher Odu, the driver from the sub-station, proffering the envelope.

The Chief's personal guard took the envelope and turned it over for inspection. Satisfied he told Odu, 'Make you wait here for small.'

Minutes later he returned. 'Chief say make you tell D.C. say him no get time for see him now. Say him get for go see him farm way, work men till, before they begin for plant yam.'

The driver left to deliver the Chief's reply to Hughes.

'Godfrey, you've arrived at last!' Adiabua exclaimed.

'Yes, I would've come sooner but I'd some odds and ends to tidy up.'

'I wouldn't have sent for you but for the fact that I've a special assignment for you. You've seen today's paper?'

'Yes, it's marvellous.'

'It's the story of the century, and Martin's baby. I must confess I wasn't very enthusiastic with the whole thing at first. However, that's not what I sent for you to tell you. I've a job for you, as I've already said, very different from the usual reporting.'

'Well, what is it?' Onyeso said eagerly.

Adiabua coughed and reshuffled some papers on his desk. 'Godfrey, I want you, for this assignment, to deny, if challenged openly, that you've any connection with the paper. If you don't know how to drink, start drinking now. You've to haunt every bar, buy drinks freely, but listen carefully. I want you to find out the men who used Agba as their shield. We know now, but we're keeping it a secret for the moment, that Josiah Agba killed Ephraim Obi, the man who was murdered in the mine. What, however, we don't know, and would like to know, is the motive behind the murder. I expect now that Agba has hanged himself, that those whose dirty job he did are sighing with relief that they'll never be found out. This is where we come in. We'll help to winkle them out. And that's where you start.'

'What!' shouted Onyeso.

Adiabua went on as though he was totally unaware of the shock and surprise on the face of his roving reporter. 'You see you're not based here, you come only once in a blue moon and therefore you're not known locally. If I sent any of the other reporters, they'd be instantly recognise, but with you that danger doesn't exist.'

'And after that, what then? Don't forget that the secret society have a way of catching up with people who tripped them up, and they never, never forgive,' Onyeso warned him.

'I'm aware of that. We won't let you fall into that danger, believe me.'

'But surely the police are doing all they can, why not let them get on with it, for heaven's sake? After all that's what they're paid for,' protested Onyeso.

'I'm aware of that too. Newspapers, however, have been known to have one of their able reporters about on a story such as this you know. It's not unusual. I've also asked the police for their full co-operation, and if the worst comes to the worst, you'll be rescued in time.'

'That's a cheerful thought, I must say!'

'You'll enjoy it once you get started!' said Adiabua, but he could not bring himself to look Onyeso in the face.

'I'm sure I shall,' Onyeso said dryly, and added, 'I've a wife and two children to think of!'

'I'm sure it won't come to that. The police will keep their part of the bargain. They're just as anxious as we are to get to the bottom of the story. Public outcry about the murder, plus their knowledge of the police's previous inefficiencies, has put up the back of every member of the force. They're going flat out now to show the public, who've seen nothing but their worst side, that they indeed have the stuff that policemen are made of!'

'I hope so!' replied Onyeso, shedding some of his worried lines. 'When d'you want me to start?'

'Immediately. I'll sign a cash voucher for you to take to the accountant. You'd better arrange a clandestine meeting place with Martin, so that you can report your progress to him each night, or whatever time is convenient to you to do so. And phone your wife that you'll be away for some time.'

'Ah, sometime when trouble come, it come with two head!' Obieze cried and shook his head.

'How you mean?' Iru, his favourite wife, who cooked his meals and had his ear and confidence, asked.

'D.C. send messenger for tell me say he want for see me.'

'So?' Iru asked, fear clutching her heart, knowing what she did.

'So I send word back through him messenger say for tell him say I busy.'

'You think that be good thing you do?' his wife asked gently.

Obieze swung round to face her. 'What you think I for do, hmm? You think I be for run hot foot for go meet him and run for inside trap?'

'No, that no be reason why I think you for go meet him. The reason why I think you for go see what D.C. want be because, that way, you go know what the man think. Now you no go know what he think because you no go. Maybe he no want anything. Maybe he just want for see you as you be new Chief.'

'No, Iru, I know what you try for do, and I glad, but you no know this people like I do. If I run go quick this time like him houseboy, he go send for me like that all the time!

101

I no go fit call me own soul me own. He go turn ruler and me go turn small boy. No, Iru, I think I do proper.'

'That be true,' his wife added, 'but my mind for rest better if we know what he think.'

'Make you no worry for that,' Obieze informed her. 'I know what he think. He think the same thing we think. But if he think say I be fool, say, I go volunteer for tell him what I know he think, he craze!'

His wife looked at him wonderingly. 'You look as if you glad for fight D.C.' But Obieze did not reply as he cast his mind back a few years to when Hughes had insulted his father for refusing to let a main road go through his father's best farming land. If the D.C. had expressed his wish in a calm and reasonable voice, his father would have understood and perhaps would have agreed to let the road go through. But no, the D.C. had shouted and raged, saying that the road must go through whether his father approved or not, because it would enable the lorries carrying palm produce to go directly to the wharf to be unloaded on to ships, instead of going a roundabout route. What galled Obieze most was that his father, the town's ruler, had been shouted at and been made to look small in front of the townspeople. The road never went through, but the memory remained indelible. Another thing, he was unwilling to have the new phenomenon of being summoned to the D.C.'s head-quarters, take root. Obieze therefore decided that he would not budge.

'I think I do proper,' he told his wife. 'If D.C. want for see me, make him come here, he get leg!'

His wife looked at him with admiration. 'Ah, you get strong head!' she teased. They smiled at each other fondly.

'Make you come close,' he told her.

She took a few steps backwards. 'No!'

'You still do . . .?'

She shook her head and blushed. 'I finish day before yesterday. I just tire.'

'How you tire? Look how you fat with all my chop you eat, and all my palm wine you hide for drink all the time! You think say, I no notice? You think say the eye way be for my head to be there for nothing?' Obieze teased her.

She chuckled. 'I no know say you watch me! Ah, you wicked!'

102

'You come close now?' he persisted.

'Small, small,' she warned him beforehand.

He ambled nearer. 'Which kind talk be that?' he boomed out at her.

'Edward,' she murmured softly, calling him by his Christian name. 'D.C. worry me.'

'Make D.C. run helter skelter go jump for inside Ujo River!' he said, dismissing the looming shadow of the District Commissioner and concentrating on the job in hand.

'Yes, what is it?' Hughes inquired over the phone.

'It's Jack Bailey here, sir.'

'Well, go on!'

'Well, sir, I've just spoken to the court interpreter at Ukana. He informs me that with regard to the invitation you sent to the Chief asking him to come and see you, the Chief said that the moment isn't propitious.'

'Meaning?' Hughes asked.

'He says that he's busy because of the approaching farming season.'

'I see,' Hughes replied quietly and went on, 'Phone Ukana again. Tell our man there that I want him to go and see Obieze again. Tell him to say that I'm aware that this is a very busy time of the year for him and I wouldn't wish to disrupt his programme, but that he'd be doing me a great favour if he came down. Or I could go up to see him, as what I wish to discuss with him is of very great importance, and very grave. Did you get that?'

'Yes, sir.'

'Good. Phone the message through right away and also tell the interpreter to phone the Chief's reply back to you without delay, as soon as he finishes with him.'

'I'll do that, sir.'

'And Bailey, if the reply doesn't come through before two this afternoon, have the operator switch all after office calls to your home. I must know the Chief's reply today. Phone it to me at home when you get it,' Hughes instructed and rang off.

'My man! Hey, you!' shouted Anako to a passer-by. When the man turned Anako asked, 'You know how for paint?'

103

'How you mean?' the passer-by asked back.

'I mean how for hold brush and put it inside bucket with chalk water.'

The man looked blank. 'Eh?' he became sufficiently aware to ask.

'How you look as if you no know nothing!' said Anako in exasperation, and then went on to enlighten him. 'When you put brush for inside chalk water, you take it come out again, and you begin for push brush up and down, up and down, up and down, until chalk water take to wall.'

'Ah,' the passer-by replied, moving closer to Anako. The explanation had sunk in.

'You think you go fit do it now?' asked Anako when the man stood face to face with him.

'I no do it before but I go try.'

'O.K. Make you come start.'

'Wait small,' said the newly hired painter. 'You no tell me how much you go pay me for the job.'

'Three pence every day until job finish.'

The man demurred. 'Ah, it small. You no fit increase pay?'

'No, the court here for Ukana be small court, we no get plenty money like they get for big court,' explained Anako.

The man looked as if the court interpreter was talking a whole load of rubbish. 'I want sixpence for the job or I no do paint.'

'All right, you get the job,' Anako told him. Considering that the farming season was upon them, he was happy to get anyone at all.

'Which place be the paint?' the man asked as he removed his robe.

'We go get the paint, but I want you go for stream first for go bring water come.'

The man stared, speechless. 'Eh? You no bin tell me say I go bring water also!' he protested after he found his voice.

'You want the job, or you no want the job?' Anako asked wearily.

'I want the job,' the man assured him. 'I just surprise about the water business. I no carry water for my head for long, long time.'

'Well, this be govment job,' said Anako to his new man.

'For govment job you do everything,' he added from the pages of his long years of service.

'Eh?'

'Ah, I talk true word. Govment job be like woman job, it no finish. You work like jackass!'

The man looked convinced. 'All right, give me bucket for go stream.'

'It be for inside that shed,' Anako replied pointing.

At that moment Eze, the night-watchman, approached to tell Anako that the phone in Mr MacIntosh's office was ringing again.

'Ah phone, phone, phone all the time, the thing no give me rest!' he wailed. He placed the new man in Eze's care and went off to see who was on the phone.

'Anako here.'

'Sorry to worry you again, Mr Anako, Bailey here.'

Anako's face creased in a smile. 'You no worry me, Mr Bailey,' he assured him.

'Good. I've another message for the Chief, but this time the District Commissioner wants you to deliver it to him yourself.'

The smile left the court interpreter's face and his face fell. 'I no fit, Mr Bailey,' he whispered.

'Why not?'

'Mr Bailey, as I bin tell Mr Jenkin and Mr Underwood this morning-time, Chief Obieze no like me.'

'That shouldn't stop you from delivering the message,' said Bailey flippantly.

Anako sighed when no support seemed to be coming from the man at the other end of the line. He tried once more, this time more explicitly. 'I no think say you understand me, Mr Bailey. Chief Obieze set trap for me.'

'In what way?'

Anako remarked in an aside to Odu, the driver, who had joined him in the office, 'He no fit follow what I tell him. They all be the same, they no understand African man him business.'

'I asked you a question, Mr Anako,' Bailey said impatiently.

Anako turned his full attention back to the phone. 'Yes, yes, Mr Bailey, I still be for here. All right I go go see Chief.'

'Then this is the message you're to deliver . . .'

Chapter Ten

To visit an African township is an adventure in itself ; to sit and partake of what it has to offer, is an experience that would last one a lifetime. The haunting guitar music with its high-life rhythm, with the evening's self-appointed soloist, wailing out from time to time the words the guitar can only twang but cannot say ; the smoke-filled room ; draught players sitting in a corner with their tumblers of palm wine, sour or fresh, depending on whether they are winning or losing the game ; this all makes up the scene. One can order any dish one wishes, or one may have dined at home and merely come for the gossip, the shouting, the heat and the sweat. The bar is illuminated with kerosene lamps, placed at strategic points. At intervals, the more sober among the revellers walk around and blow at the fluttering insects around the lamps, in case they singe themselves.

It was on such a night that Godfrey Onyeso, the region's chief reporter for *The Daily Observer*, set out for a bar to see what information he could gather for his paper about the events that necessitated Josiah Agba hanging himself after murdering a fellow miner.

Onyeso's first stop was at the Sunshine Bar in the centre of town which was heavily patronised by traders and some important business men. Any news that was news at all reached this bar first, then on to the *Observer*, then the police and finally the general public.

Onyeso eased his way towards the female bartender, 'A large bottle of fresh palm wine and tumbler, please,' he told her and waited. He looked about him and then brought his eyes back to the counter, impatient to be served.

The hard eyes and knowing smile of the woman bartender first looked at the money that Onyeso threw down on the counter, and then at Onyeso with invitation clearly written all over her face. When Onyeso made it clear there was nothing doing as far as rumping was concerned, the woman darted quickly to the rows of bottled palm wine stacked at the far end of the counter. Onyeso carried his wine and tumbler in search of a vacant seat.

'I've never seen you here before,' said a small man dressed in shorts and shirt, who Onyeso now sat next to.

'No, I'm new here.'

'Ah, you have just arrived in the region,' said the man, looking a little tipsy.

'Yes,' Onyeso told him and drained half his tumbler of palm wine.

'Where do you come from?'

'From the coast.'

'I see,' said Onyeso's companion, who seemed satisfied for the moment. They drank in silence for a whole, before the reporter, in a roundabout way, launched into the subject that had brought him to the bar.

'It's terrible for anyone to hang himself!' Onyeso exclaimed, and threw up his hands.

'Too terrible,' sighed his drinking companion, and went on, 'I knew the man very well.'

The reporter pricked up his ears. 'Oh?' he murmured casually as if he was already losing interest in the subject.

His companion nodded. 'I knew Josiah even though I don't work in the mine. The man was as quiet as a snail. He never talked too much, but he drank like hell!'

'Oh?' repeated Onyeso, even more casually.

'What surprised me was why Josiah agreed to do what he did.'

'What did he do?' Onyeso asked as if he didn't know what Agba had done besides hanging himself. He swivelled round to look at the man seated next to him full in the face.

'Cut the throat of his brother miner when the latter was about to leave the pithead after work.'

'But I heard before I left the coast, that the whole thing about the murder was a lie; that it was an accident; that coal fell on the dead man's head. That was the cause of his death,' contributed Onyeso.

His companion put down the full tumbler of wine he was about to set to his lips, with a thump, and began to jab his fore-finger into Onyeso's chest as he spoke. 'No!' he shouted. 'I come from this region, and I know what happened. It wasn't an accident. Coal didn't fall on Ephraim Obi's head. Ephraim Obi died, because he knew too much!' He paused and took a long draught from his palm wine. 'My friend, if you ask me the reason why Ephraim Obi was murdered, I will say it's because he knew that the secret society people killed his father in the mine two years ago. And it was all because his father was the foreman at the mine. The secret society people are against anyone who isn't one of their number being the foreman at the mine.'

'I see,' replied Onyeso as he took the detail in.

'But people are afraid to tell the police,' his companion told him, and wiped perspiration from his eyes.

'Who are the members of the secret society?' asked Onyeso. His companion looked at him with startled eyes, then lowered his.

'I don't know,' he mumbled. 'Even if I knew, I couldn't tell you. It's dangerous to tell on them.'

'Come on, tell me,' said Onyeso in his assumed casual tone and manner, and with a smile that did not touch his eyes. Seeing that the man, after some seconds, was not going to tell him, Onyeso went on, 'I don't care if you don't want to tell me. I'm from another region, and couldn't care less about the whole thing.'

These facts seemed somehow to penetrate to Onyeso's companion and take hold, for the man said with a smile, 'Of course, I'd forgotten that. I'd forgotten that you're not from this region.'

'Did you think if I came from this region that I would've asked you? I would've known the facts myself,' Onyeso said logically.

'That's extremely doubtful because you wouldn't have known the inside story I just told you. Only two or three people who work in the mine know.'

'I see,' said Onyeso, and waited.

'What are you doing here in Utuka?' the man asked abruptly.

Onyeso thought quickly. 'I came to buy small articles for trade.'

'Same here,' the man supplied. 'It's always nice to meet someone in the same profession,' he added with a big smile.

Onyeso smiled back, and began to breathe more easily.

'What sort of things have you come to buy and sell when you get back to the coast?' the man shot at Onyeso unexpectedly.

Onyeso paused slightly to think. 'Looking glass, combs,

silko thread, exercise books. Things like that,' said Onyeso, and wiped the sudden perspiration that broke out on his forehead.

His drinking companion chuckled. He had noticed Onyeso's slight hesitation. 'My dear man,' he said at last. 'You are not trader. Your hands aren't like the hands of a man who handles petty cash. If you are a trader as you just said, you wouldn't have stopped to think about what you came to buy. My friend, the cigarette you're smoking, no petty trader would be able to afford it. My dear man, you work in an office. Your English is much too good. I speak good English myself, but not as well as you. Yours is much too good for a trader!'

Onyeso sat stunned. His companion's eyes held his as a cobra holds its prey before it strikes.

Onyeso sat bereft of words. His companion laughed softly and went on, 'As soon as I saw you enter the bar, I said to myself, "That man is not accustomed to entering this sort of bar, even though he's an African". There are Africans and Africans, if you know what I mean!'

Onyeso sat numbed. He thought he had had it.

The man sipped from his palm wine and wiped his mouth with the back of his hand, and without looking at Onyeso queried, 'Who sent you? What do you want to know?'

Those questions aroused Onyeso and without giving much thought to what he would reply he said flatly, 'I want you to tell me the names of the members of the secret society.'

The man smiled again. 'Do you want the names of the big fish, or the small fish?'

'The big fish,' Onyeso told him.

His companion paused to think it over in his mind. 'If I tell you, what will you do with them?'

'Nothing. I just want to know,' said Onyeso airily.

The man looked fed up. 'My dear man!' he shouted in disgust. 'Speak the truth. You work in an office. Who sent you? The Government?'

'I don't work for the Government,' Onyeso replied, and his drinking friend gazed into Onyeso's eyes and thought he read truth there.

'All right,' said the man. 'I believe that you're not employed by the Government. Who's your employer?'

This time Onyeso was more agile in his thinking. 'I work

for The Amalgamated Construction Company,' he lied without hesitation. 'I'm their accountant.'

The man looked at him and smiled once more. 'So I was right in not believing that you're a trader,' he said with the arrogance of one who knows he has a far superior intuition and knowledge than he was credited for.

'Yes, you were right,' Onyeso agreed with feigned humility, and the lump in his throat began to go down.

'Why did you lie to me about your job in the first place?' asked the other fellow with a touch of reprimand in his voice.

'I wanted to know you better, and try you out, before telling you the nature of my job,' lied Onyeso again.

'I see. But what does the Construction Company want with the secret society?' the man wanted to know. He and Onyeso hardly touched their palm wine now, so deep was their rapport.

'The company wants to invest a large sum of money in the mine. But they're reluctant to do so if the miners are bent on killing each other. They want the place cleaned out first of the secret society.'

'But why didn't you give me this information before, from the very beginning? It would've made things easier. Why lie, before telling the truth?'

'As I've just pointed out to you, I didn't know you that well before. You can't expect me to say all this to a complete stranger? Think it over, and you'll see my point,' Onyeso reasoned.

They stared into each other's eyes. The other man's were shining with respect.

'You were being cautious?' said Onyeso's companion.

'Yes, I have to be, with the sort of errand entrusted to me.'

The man looked at Onyeso with open admiration. 'You have good head on your shoulder,' he pronounced finally.

Onyeso, trying to be modest, violently disagreed with the compliment. But he said, 'Thank you,' nevertheless.

'Does all the company's money go through your hands' the man asked in wonder. 'A young man like you?' he added.

Onyeso quickly corrected any wrong impression he may have given. 'No. Not all the company's money. Just some.'

But as the subject of money always held immense interest to both young and old, rich and poor, alike, one could imagine what it did to the trader whose sole object in life was to amass and hoard it. It went beyond reason. 'How much do you handle each day?' he wanted to know.

Onyeso was secretly amused, in spite of himself, at what he suspected was going on in the stranger's mind. 'Very little,' he said, hoping this would put a stop to any hope the stranger might be entertaining of calling him in at some time in the future as an accomplice to break in and rob the supposed company he worked for. This however did not deter his companion.

'But sometimes you handle big money just for a second,' the man told Onyeso.

Onyeso said yes as he did not want to deny the man all illusions of him, however false.

'Petty trading is very bad now,' the man was saying, as he scratched his head. 'I have one son in secondary school; three in elementary school; three wives; two are pregnant at the moment. Things are difficult for me at the moment,' he said to Onyeso with a sidelong glance.

'How much do you want for the information I want from you?' Onyeso inquired, hoping this would put a stop to any further hard luck stories from the man.

His drinking companion gave a short laugh that did not come from the heart. 'It isn't how much I want; it's how much you're prepared to give me.'

'Three pounds?' Onyeso suggested.

The man shut his eyes and laughed hard and long. It was too funny for words. When he could laugh no more he opened his eyes, cleared his throat, and told Onyeso coldly. 'Three pounds isn't money. I want something more tangible to put away in the bank. I told you only a minute ago, that I've family worries. What could I possibly do with three pounds? Pay school fees? Or see my wives through pregnancy?'

Onyeso increased the amount. 'Five pounds,' he said.

His stout short companion breathed in and out and started to brush something that looked to him like a speck of dust from his shorts. 'I want fifty pounds,' he said, still busily brushing off the speck of dust with singular concentration.

111

'What!' Onyeso shouted. He was about to say more but the man cut him short.

'Speak quietly,' was the other man's advice. 'Do you want the rest of the people to hear us?'

'I'll give you ten pounds,' Onyeso told him, pretending to get up from his seat as he was fed up with wrangling over money.

'Sit down!' the man ordered him. 'Twenty-five pounds, and I want it in currency. I don't want a cheque. You never can tell, there might be some secret society people working in the bank. I don't want to get into trouble.'

'I see,' replied Onyeso. 'I'll give you ten pounds in cash.'

'No, twenty-five,' said the man.

'Fifteen,' replied Onyeso, on his feet now.

'Sit down! I'll take it!'

Onyeso sat down. 'I'll give you the money tomorrow night beside the thirty mile limit sign outside the township.'

'And I'll give you the names when you give me the money.'

Onyeso and the man drained their tumblers, shook hands and stood up to leave.

'Eight o'clock?' Onyeso asked his companion.

The stout short would-be informer nodded. 'At eight o'clock sharp.'

They parted.

Bailey was standing by the window in Mason's office when the phone rang.

'Jack Bailey,' he said.

'Mr Bailey, I see Chief,' Anako informed him from Ukana.

The junior secretary pulled out Mason's chair and sat down. 'Yes, what did he say?'

'He say he no fit come to Utuka for see D.C. at all. He get too much business for hand. He say, maybe D.C. no get plenty work to do. If that be the case, make D.C. come here to Ukana for see him. Obieze also say, ordinary D.C. no get power to summon him up and down region like if he be small boy.'

Bailey was about to laugh but checked himself in time. 'I see,' he said. 'Well, I'll pass on the Chief's reply to the District Commissioner.'

'All right, Mr Bailey.'

They both rang off.

'Well! Hughes won't like this!' laughed Bailey after he put down the receiver. 'How the dickens am I going to relate this message to him,' he wondered. 'I daren't risk delivering it to him in person. I'll pass it along, as he said, over the phone.' Still laughing he picked up the receiver and dialled Hughes at home.

'What did you say he said?' shouted Hughes over the phone, when Bailey had finished.

'What I've just told you, sir?'

'Was he drunk?'

Bailey coughed to stop himself from bursting at the sides. 'I don't know, sir. I'm just repeating what the court interpreter said over the phone.'

'Obieze's showing provocative obstinacy!' said Hughes testily. When Bailey made no reply, Hughes asked: 'Where are you phoning from? Home or office?'

'From the office. I know it's after office hours, but I thought I'd wait here a bit longer, just in case, and it's only a few minutes after half past two.'

'I see,' Hughes replied, and went on to complain. 'You must realise that the Chief's reply is derisory,' he pointed out, as if Bailey was to blame.

'I agree, sir.'

That seemed to comfort Hughes a little. 'Look, Bailey, send word back to our man there. Tell him that I said he must tell Obieze this. Are you listening carefully?'

'Yes, sir.'

'You'd better fetch paper and pencil to take it down.'

Bailey reached for pencil and paper. 'I'm ready, sir.'

'Tell him to say this to the Chief. Crop or no crop; busy or not; whether I'm the Governor or not – I want to see him here tomorrow morning at ten!'

'Yes, sir.'

Onyeso, the reporter for the *Observer*, walked out from the Sunshine Bar and into the cool night air. He stood for a minute to inhale the fresh breeze and then began to walk in the direction of the room he had booked in town for the duration of his assignment.

'Godfrey!' came a voice out of nowhere.

Onyeso sobered up and looked about him in despair. Who,

he asked himself, could be addressing him by his first name? Who else besides his colleagues at the *Observer* knew him here? He was helped out of his dilemma when the voice whispered again. 'This way, it's Martin!'

Onyeso sighed with relief and walked in the direction of the voice.

'How did you get on?' asked Martin Ofodile, the news editor.

'Not bad,' replied Onyeso and could not help adding, 'but, Martin, we did arrange to meet at midnight at the lane behind my lodgings. It's not that time yet. However,' Onyeso sighed, 'I'll have something concrete for you tomorrow night. Meet me at the thirty mile limit sign on the road out of town, just before eight. I have a rendezvous with someone there at eight. Bring fifteen pounds with you in cash. I'd like you to stay there with me, out of sight but not out of hearing, until my interview with the man finishes.'

'Who is he, what's his name?'

'I don't know, I didn't ask his name. All I know is that he's a trader and is willing, for fifteen pounds, to give me the information we want. He sounded genuine enough, I'm sure his information will be accurate. Anyway, we'll find out about all that tomorrow.'

'You must try and get his name and address when you meet in case we want to contact him again,' the news editor told him.

'But informers here are always reluctant to give their names and addresses until they know you better,' Onyeso reminded him.

'Tell him that it'll be all right this time, that he needn't worry. As soon as this matter ends, we'll have no further use for him, because it's a very important case. We'll no longer need him, or he us.'

'All right, I'll try, but I won't promise anything,' Onyeso said, and went on his way.

Obieze surveyed the dinner put before him of garri and okoro soup, and pushed it aside. 'If it be trouble D.C. want, then I go give him trouble!' he raged.

'But I bin think say, trouble with D.C. finish?' his wife asked him as she came out to join him from the inner sanctum.

Obieze sighed. 'So me also bin think. But it no look as if to say the man think so. I think he want make what happen to Mr Mason happen to him!'

'Ah, make you no talk so,' his wife reprimanded gently. 'That kind thing no good for happen all the time.'

Obieze spread his hands in perplexity. 'What you want make I do, hmm?'

'I think if he say make you see him, make you do so,' she advised. 'Maybe, he no want for see you because of the thing you do to Mr Mason.'

'What he want see me for then?' he asked. When she did not reply he continued, 'You think he just want to look me for face and pat my head?'

His wife suppressed her urge to say something equally annoying, as she realised that in her husband's present mood it would be unwise. Instead she told him, 'You be new Chief, maybe he just want make you and him meet.'

Obieze shook his wise head. 'No, Iru, something worry D.C. If he bin just want for see me, he for wait and we see each other when he come for ordinary trek. But as he send message three time for one day, the palaver he want see me about, big. And him first message say, what he want to see me about, strong and deep.'

'Aaaah,' Iru replied, looking at him comprehendingly.

They stood and looked at each other for a while. There was no need for words. The telegraphic communication between husband and wife transmitted all that needed to be said. But as his wife looked frightened about what they both knew, he felt he needed to ease her fears. 'Make you lef everything for my hand. He go soon tire for send message if I turn deaf ear to him! My father bin get plenty trouble from D.C. too, so this no be new thing.'

'But when your father live, no D.O. die,' she reminded him. 'All this trouble no reach me and you before, when your father be Chief.'

'Well, I be Chief now, that be the reason. When you be Chief, you get Chief trouble. When you be ordinary man, you get ordinary man trouble. Life not steady anymore. It go up and down, up and down, all the time. Sometime, for my heart, I want to wake up and no be Chief at all. Then I say to myself ; if I no be Chief, who go be Chief?'

'That be true. What you have, you no want. What you no have, you want.'

'World hard now,' Obieze mused, his mind far away. 'When my grandfather be Chief, world stand still. All the trouble with D.C. begin to come when my father be Chief. And it no looks as if it go stop.'

He waved his wife, who was about to speak, to silence and continued, 'I want all my children go school for learn book because many things begin for change!'

His wife looked at him in astonishment.

'It be true,' he told her softly, and with a faint smile. 'I want my first son, Anyagu, to go England for finish school because plenty change, plenty trouble, go come,' he said, walking up and down the medium sized room.

'And the money?' his wife asked.

'That no worry me. I get some for hand now. And after we plant and harvest crop, I go get plenty more. I no know, Iru, I no know. Something inside me tell me say, to send Anyagu to England now-now.'

His wife looked at him wonderingly.

'Are you busy, Michael?'

'No, not really.'

'I've brought the proofs for tomorrow's paper,' Ofodile said and waited for a junior reporter to finish with the editor before launching into the real reason, besides bringing the dummy, why he wanted to see the editor. After the junior reporter had left Ofodile said, 'I saw Godfrey.'

Adiabua looked at him sharply, 'Well?'

'He's already made contact,' Ofodile told him and paused.

'Well, go on!' said Adiabua impatiently.

'I'm to meet him tomorrow night with fifteen pounds in my pocket.'

'That's rather a lot!'

'It's the amount Godfrey requested.'

'And he's certain we'll get the right information after we've paid up?'

'So he thinks. We'd better let the police in on this.'

'Yes, I'll do that in a minute,' replied Adiabua looking at his telephone. 'Which reminds me, I phoned the District Commissioner this morning about the missing District Officer but didn't get anywhere with him.'

116

'Have you ever known anyone get anywhere with that man?' Ofodile asked dryly.

'Since it was Godfrey who telephoned in the story, I'm sure it's accurate.'

'Yes, I'm certain it is. If it weren't for this mine murder affair, I'd have made it the lead story and annoyed that D.C.'

Adiabua looked at his watch, it said half past nine. 'It's late now.'

'To ring him again and give him one more chance, or to use the story as the second lead?'

'To ring him generally. They're not like us you know, working from morning till never, never. They knock off at two!'

'There's nothing stopping us from ringing his home,' Ofodile argued.

'Yes, I know but ...'

'Let's give it a try,' said Ofodile mischievously. 'Everyone's allowed to be offensive once. Besides, we're only doing our duty and our job, and anyway, it's time he learned that the cards are stacked high on our side!'

'Sometimes, Martin, you make be look tame. I suppose being the editor has removed some of the fire from my belly!' They laughed as Adiabua lifted the receiver and placed a call to the home of the District Commissioner, Utuka, the region's headquarters.

'There'll be an hour's delay, sir,' the operator told him.

'I'll wait,' he said and hung up. He turned to Ofodile. 'Let's go through with the page proofs while we wait.'

'I'd particularly like you to see the pictures in the centre pages. While you're looking at them, I'll get some more.'

Minutes later he was back.

Adiabua eyed the pictures. 'It's too late for those now, the engraving department has closed.'

'I was thinking about their future use,' replied the news editor.

Adiabua glanced at them more fully. 'Hmm, this new photographer is very good. Where did you say he worked before?'

'In some studio, I forget which. He's certainly better than the one we had before, that one couldn't even focus his lens!'

Adiabua stared at him and shook his head helplessly. 'Let the picture editor have them, and while you're about it, send someone down to ask the works manager how he's coping.'

He had barely finished speaking when his phone rang. 'Yes?'

'Please hold the line for Utuka.'

'But I thought you told me there'd be an hour's delay,' said Adiabua, annoyed at being interrupted from seeing the page proofs through.

'Yes, sir, but we got through much quicker than expected.'

'Oh, well,' he said and motioned the news editor to listen on another phone in an adjoining office.

'Hughes speaking.'

'The editor of the *Observer* here.'

'But I thought I'd said all that's to be said on the matter.'

'You said nothing,' Adiabua told him calmly.

'So what d'you intend to do about it?'

'Spread the story right across the front page!' he said, with a wink at Ofodile in the next room.

'And I'll sue you for libel,' Hughes countered.

'There're ways of jiggling a story to save it from being libellous.'

Hughes fumed. 'Now look here!'

'You look here!'

'I'm warning you, if that story gets on your front page, or anywhere in the paper for that matter, I'll take it up with whoever's your proprietor and you'll find yourself in a very sticky position indeed!'

'You can take it as high as you wish, and let me tell you this, I don't respond favourably with a gun in my back. By all means go and see the proprietor if you wish!' There was a pause. 'Are you still with me?' Adiabua asked.

'Yes, of course I'm still with you. Where d'you think I am!'

'Well? Are you going to co-operate, or do you intend to remain on your high horse?'

'My dear fellow, I won't have you speak to me like that!'

'We could be very friendly, you know, if you'd only let us.'

'But your paper has always been unkind to us.'

'In what way?'

118

'You've always mis-quoted me and you damn well know it!'

'If we have, we've been goaded into doing so.'

'I dare say!'

'As regards the missing D.O. . . .'

'Yes, what about him?'

'So he is missing then!' Adiabua had trapped him.

'There you go again! I never said that!'

'But it's obvious.'

'The man must have lost his way while on trek . . .'

Adiabua cut him short. 'After being in this region for fifteen years? Where everyone knows him? That's not possible.'

'But the impossible does happen. However, look, hold your fire for the moment regarding this matter.'

'I take it you're worried and want the minimum of fuss.'

'Yes.'

'But why didn't you say so when I rang you before?'

'I wasn't sure then, in fact I'm still not sure.'

'You'd be much happier if we left the story for the time being?'

'That would be greatly appreciated, believe me,' murmured Hughes, climbing down.

'You see how very friendly and understanding we can be!'

'Don't rub it in!'

'I'll hear from you when you know one way or the other?'

'Yes, and get what's-his-name here off my back!'

'Godfrey . . . ?'

'That's him. He's done nothing but snoop around. I'm sure he's the one who put you on to me. Where he got the story from, I don't know.'

'That's what he's paid to do.'

'There're better paid jobs.'

'Such as?'

'Never mind. Goodbye!'

'Well,' said Ofodile as he came back into the editor's office, 'he's most certainly everything I've heard he is.'

'And more,' Adiabua added. 'He has a belly full of self-importance. Shall we get on wih what we were doing?' he asked, leafing through the page proofs.

'Who was that on the phone?' asked Mrs Hughes coming into the lounge.

'Someone from the paper. They've caught on to Maurice. I put them off for the time being, though how long I'll be able to do that, I don't know.'

'Are you sure Maurice is alive?'

'What makes you think he's dead?' Hughes asked, looking at his wife steadily.

'Oh, I don't know, it's just a feeling I have.'

'Well?'

'A grown man getting lost, it seems rather odd.'

'It does happen you know. Getting lost isn't only the prerogative of children.'

'What I mean is, expatriates don't just amble off, not here at any rate.'

'They do you know. Think of all the missionaries that get lost!'

'But with Maurice it's different. He knows this place like the back of his hand.'

'I know, that's what surprises me too. Maybe he's just doing this deliberately. It's just the sort of thing he'd do – anything for a lark! I've hardly got MacIntosh off my hands, and now this!'

'It's such an awful bother,' said Mrs Hughes, picking up her knitting.

'I just don't know what to make of it. If I don't find him now, it'll be difficult when the rains start,' he moaned.

Mrs Hughes looked up from her knitting. 'D'you think it'll stretch that far?'

'Who knows? I certainly don't!' He stood up and yawned. 'We may as well turn in.'

Mrs Hughes's lips tightened. 'I'm not quite ready yet, there're one or two things I want to do.'

'Such as?'

She looked at him with half of her left eyebrow raised. He caught the point. 'Sorry, dear, it was just a slip of the tongue.' He paused and asked in a most unusual voice for him, 'Can't you forget that picture incident? It isn't as if I've committed adultery. I'm only human you know.'

'Are you?' she asked sarcastically, 'It's a funny admission coming from you!'

'One does make mistakes . . .'

120

Mrs Hughes's knitting needles clinked loudly. 'You're becoming a bore. I suggest you go to bed. I shan't run away. I won't do anything that would be detrimental to your lofty position, but I'll no longer be bullied!'

'Thank you, dear,' he replied as he walked off with his tail between his legs.

Chapter Eleven

Hughes stood bare-headed on his sun-baked porch and looked out at the expatriate houses and, far beyond them, the shanty town of Utuka. Previously the view had always given him a feeling of power and great satisfaction, but this morning it irked him. He had the feeling that something, unless he controlled it quickly, was about to swallow him up. What is it? he asked himself over and over again. It was through no fault of his that he made the decision to send MacIntosh home. The man was sick. And it certainly was not his fault that Maurice had disappeared. He hadn't sent him on an errand. The missing man had not informed him that he was going anywhere, which was without precedent, as every official not only notified him but discussed the project, which necessitated a trek, with him before he set out. He felt as if a rug was being pulled in a zigzag manner from under his feet. Who is pulling it, he wondered? All his life he had been able to control events, instead of letting them control him. 'The open I can fight,' he said out loud. 'The secretive I don't know how to tackle, but I'll try, even if I die in the attempt! And on top of all this I'm having my hands full with Millicent as well.'

He walked down his verandah steps carefully avoiding his wife's potted plants that lined both sides of it, and on to a tarred path in front of his garden, flanked by beautifully kept lawns.

'Jacob,' he called to their steward who had suddenly come into view. 'Tell the madam that I'm off to the office.'

'I'll walk this morning,' he said to his driver who had sprung to attention as Hughes neared the car.

'I'll bring the car for office?'

'Yes.'

"Isn't he there?'

'No,' replied Bailey to Jenkins's question.

They were standing in the main corridor of the office building. Bailey went on, 'He sent yet another message to the Chief telling him to meet him here at ten this morning. The reply has just come in.'

'George will never learn,' said Jenkins, shaking his head. 'He has a thing about seeing people at ten. You'd think there were no other numbers on the face of the clock!'

Bailey smiled at this.

'Is the Chief coming down?' Jenkins asked.

'I'm afraid his reply is negative.'

'That won't please George,' said Jenkins in mock alarm.

'Afraid not,' Bailey replied, trying desperately to keep a straight face at his colleague's antics.

'And you're the bearer of evil tidings?' Jenkins muttered.

Bailey sighed. 'Correct again.'

'I wish you luck!'

'I'll need it.'

'He's walking this morning,' Jenkins said, looking down the length of the corridor into which Hughes had just emerged through a small door. 'He always walks to the office when he's angry or perplexed. I wonder which of the two moods he's in this morning. He finds his car too cramped when he's in either mood. I think claustrophobia's the word.'

'Oh?' Bailey asked and was about to ask more when Jenkins said, 'See you later,' and disappeared into his own office.

'Good morning, sir, I've . . .' Bailey began when Hughes neared him.

'Let's go into my office, shall we?'

'Of course, sir.' A messenger opened the door and Hughes went in with Bailey following. Hughes sat behind his enormous desk and ceremoniously lifted and put down paperweights, pens and various other objects. 'Well?' he finally looked up to ask.

Bailey was sure that five minutes had elapsed, he cleared his throat. 'I've heard from Ukana about the message . . .'

'Well, well, go on, give me the message,' said Hughes impatiently.

'The Chief says he won't come.'

'That he's busy or that he won't come? There's a difference, my dear boy,' said Hughes trying to disbelieve what he'd just heard.

'That he won't come, sir,' said Bailey, feeling like a fool.

'Oh! What seems to be the matter? Is it that he's too prescient to attend?'

'He didn't stipulate, sir. What I've just told you was all he said.'

'In that case I'll attend him!'

Bailey stared in disbelief. He found it difficult at the moment to fit his senior officer back into his former well-known attitudes. Was the high and mighty Hughes climbing down? Bailey was further stupefied when Hughes went on to say in a hitherto unsuspected emollient mood, 'There's a saying here that goes something like this: "When two people are engaged in a game of hide and seek, and the other doesn't give his playmate a chance to do the hiding instead of always the running about, the wronged playmate should seize the selfish playmate by the throat and demand to know why he's been denied a turn!" Obieze has had his turn in the ring and I, the wronged playmate as it were, have thrown my hat in to demand a turn!'

'By jove!' muttered Bailey and wiped his eyes. 'When he deigns to employ his other unsuspected side, he can be charming.' He wished that Hughes would always be like this instead of his other self.

'We shall attend Obieze, you and I!'

'You wish to take me, sir?' asked Bailey, shocked.

'And why not. You're a civil servant, aren't you?'

'But I'm only a junior secretary, sir,' he blurted protestingly.

'Those senior to you aren't much better either, I should know, believe me!' Hughes told him, but he seemed to be speaking more to himself. 'My confrontation with the Chief will enrich your experience,' he added.

'I'm sure it will, sir.'

'Well, what are you waiting for? Go and get ready. We'll leave . . .' he looked at his watch, 'in thirty minutes.'

'Yes, sir.'

As Bailey left Hughes's office he almost collided with Jenkins in his haste.

'What's the matter and what are you grinning all over for?'

'I can't stop now, I can't tell you yet.'

'Well that's a fine bit of news,' Jenkins said with surprise, his tone stopping Bailey in his flight.

'Mark, I'm in an awful hurry, I'm off to Ukana with the D.C. I'll tell you all about it when I get back!' With that he dashed away leaving Jenkins staring after him with his mouth hanging open.

'I thought I heard your voice in the corridor,' Hughes said as he noiselessly opened and shut his office door.

'Hmmm?' mumbled Jenkins without thinking. He quickly corrected himself when he saw who it was. 'I'm sorry, George, I didn't realise it was you.'

'I'm going to Ukana and I'm taking Bailey with me. I sent several messages to Obieze to come and see me and he declined, so I'm going to call on him.'

'I see. D'you want me to come along as well?'

'No, that won't be necessary, I shall be back just after two. If I don't, you know where to look for me!' And with that Hughes left.

'Ali,' he called to his driver, 'have we enough petrol in the car to take us to Ukana and back?'

'No, sir,' replied his uniformed driver.

'Better fill up the tank then and meet me in front of the house. Before you come, pick up Mr Bailey at his home. If he's not there, find him.'

Hughes retraced his way to his home. 'I'm off to Ukana,' he told his wife as he shuffled some papers on the desk in his lounge. 'I shan't be away all day, I'll probably be back just after two.' He had hardly finished speaking when his car drew up. 'Well I'm off,' he added and left.

'Are you ready for the adventure?' he asked with a twinkle in his eyes as he got into the back seat. 'I don't bite you know. I suggest you come in the back,' he told Bailey, who was sitting with the driver.

'Yes, sir!' grinned Bailey as he shot out of the front seat.

'At least one of us is cheerful,' said Hughes as the junior secretary joined him. 'You've been to Ukana before?'

'Yes, sir,' replied Bailey as he made himself comfortable. 'With Bill Underwood.'

'Oh yes, of course. Both of you placed the stones that later did the vanishing act.'

'Yes, sir,' Bailey replied not knowing what other answer to give.

'Well let's go and see exactly what happened to them, shall we?' Hughes remarked with what Bailey thought to be a mischievous smile. If it hadn't been so early in the day, Bailey would have sworn that the man had had a glass or two of whisky, for Hughes's attitude, from the time Bailey went into his office to deliver the Chief's reply, to the time they sat in the car, was so unlike him.

'I'd no idea the stones had gone, sir,' commented Bailey by way of starting a conversation.

'They have, and we're going to see where they walked to!'

'I see, sir.'

Chief Obieze sat in his audience chamber surrounded by hangers-on and others who had come to seek his advice or to lay a complaint. Suddenly he heard blows from cow horns, the signal that always meant that invasion was imminent, or that a visitor extraordinary was to call on him. His blood ran cold as he stood up rigidly to wait. Those about him did not miss the signal, they too sprang to their feet and clustered around Obieze.

Hughes had first stopped at the native court to pick up the court interpreter who would convey to Obieze what the District Commissioner had come to say. From the moment Anako sat in the front seat beside the driver, the movement of the company of four had been blown every few yards from one informer's cow horn to the other, and down the line.

Obieze had deemed it necessary since receiving three successive messages from Hughes on the previous day, to line the bushes on either side of the main road discreetly with his spies, with the instructions that they were to signal him should the extraordinary, in the person of Hughes, appear. By this means, if the inevitable happened, he was not going to be caught off guard.

As Hughes's car drew up outside Obieze's gate the Chief

appeared to be more in control of himself. He told the men about him to sit down. Only he and his interpreter stood and watched the District Commissioner, with his entourage, get out of the car to begin the long walk from the gate to the centre of the compound where the Chief waited. Hughes was flanked on either side by Bailey and Mr Anako. On Obieze's face, as the three approached, was at first feigned surprise that gave way to an intimidating smile. Hughes did not miss either and ignored both.

'Your Highness,' Hughes began, 'I found myself here in your township and thought it would be discourteous of me if I were to leave without calling on you.'

To this Obieze inclined his head with a guileful smile. Hughes' and Obieze's eyes sparkled into each other's. Who is fooling who? they asked themselves, each conscious of the assaying glance, the unspoken, probing assessment beneath the contrived polite surface.

Hughes eyed him and went on, 'I sent messages to you yesterday suggesting a meeting, but your Highness wasn't in favour, or rather was indisposed to any meeting.' Hughes made an indication with his head and Anako picked up his cue.

'Mr District Commissioner say, him sent word say, him want for see you, but you tell him say, you no fit.'

Obieze's own interpreter passed the message into the Chief's left ear which was slightly inclined towards him. The Chief mumbled his reply and his man told Anako the gist of it.

'Chief Obieze say,' continued Anako, 'it no be true say, him no want for come. Say, when you first send word say, you want for see him, him tell you say, him get plenty business for hand. He further say, you yourself know say, this be busy time for everybody because rain go soon come and everybody want for begin plant crop.'

Hughes nodded at this and went on to say, 'I see, but please inform the Chief that what I wanted to see him about wouldn't have taken more than ten minutes.'

'Chief Obieze, Mr District Commissioner say, what him want for see you, no for reach ten minute.'

Obieze intoned a reply to his man, and Anako picked it up. 'Mr District Commissioner, Chief say, you for give somebody what be inside message for give him if the message no long as you say. He say also, him no fit journey all the way for Utuka for just ten minute chat.'

'The matter was of a confidential nature as I pointed out to the Chief in my second message. That was the reason why I wanted to speak to him personally, instead of revealing it to a go-between, however trusted.'

'D.C. say what him want for tell you, him no bin want make anybody hear the thing,' interrupted Anako.

Obieze rambled further and the court interpreter translated, 'Chief Obieze say, you for tell him so, for first place.'

'It doesn't matter now,' said Hughes, anxious to end this particular exchange in order to embrace the real reason why he came. 'As we've at last met,' he continued, 'ask the Chief whether he's seen or heard anything about the District Officer of this region, Mr Mason?'

'Chief, D.C. say, you see or hear something way connect to D.O.'

Obieze paused before passing on his reply.

'Chief say, how you mean, Mr District Commissioner?' interpreted Anako.

'The D.O. came here last week, and since Sunday I've neither heard nor seen anything of him,' Hughes explained.

'D.C. say him D.O. loss since he come here for Ukana.'

This information brought a wave of murmur from the onlookers in the audience chamber. Obieze looked at Hughes innocently as he gave his reply.

'Chief say, him no know D.O. loss. Say him sorry for hear D.O. loss.'

'So am I.' Hughes replied dryly and went on: 'What I also want to find out is how the stones my men placed at strategic points on the main road as marks, disappeared overnight.'

'Mr District Commissioner want for know for which place all the rockery him mans put for road go?'

Obieze looked annoyed and turned to his man and violently expostulated. 'Mr D.C., Chief say how him go know for which place rockery go? Say, you talk to him as if he be road sweeper,' said Anako.

'On the contrary, Your Highness, my question wasn't meant to imply that at all. I can assure you that I've never thought of you in that way. My main aim for asking you the question was that perhaps one of your men may've seen the stones being playfully removed by someone who'd not attached any importance to them, and having witnessed the incident, may've casually mentioned it to you in the course of conversation.'

Amusement touched the corners of Bailey's mouth as he listened to the exchanges taking place, the first he had witnessed.

'D.C. say maybe somebody take rockery come out for road?'

Obieze shrugged his massive shoulders, and the court interpreter interpreted it as, 'perhaps'.

Obieze added something more through his man and Anako voiced it to Hughes. 'Mr D.C., Chief Obieze say, rockery no get right for stay for road.'

'I quite agree,' Hughes admitted and continued, 'In that case, as I suggested earlier, someone must have removed them as presumably they may have caused an obstruction.'

'Mr D.C. say, maybe rockery give trouble.'

Obieze shrugged his shoulders once more and Anako interpreted it as 'maybe'.

At this stage intense whispering started among those in the audience chamber. Obieze turned and gestured for quiet, and the crowd became still again. Hughes used the Chief's temporary distraction to ask his next torrent of questions intending to, and catching, Obieze unawares, though he quickly recovered.

'Who, Your Highness, removed them? Who instructed those that did, to do so?'

Almost peremptorily Obieze addressed Anako, but his eyes were on Hughes.

'Chief say make you no ask him vexing question. Say, how him go know? Say, him get other thing for do for worry for who take, or no take, rockery come out for road!'

'All right, please tell him I'll find out who the culprits are, and that when I do, I'll deal severely with them and that I'll also deal with whoever put the idea into their heads!' said Hughes furiously.

Obieze swayed imperceptibly forward, a strange expression fleetingly manifested itself in the large but otherwise perpetually passive face. He bypassed his own interpreter this time and gave his reply directly to Anako. 'Chief say, who you think you talk to, so?'

128

Hughes, who had caught the fleeting expression on Obieze's face and had since been watching him wonderingly, replied with unstinting boldness, 'Tell him, Mr Anako, that I'm very much aware whom I'm addressing, and that fact increases the seriousness of the matter. Indeed, the fact that I've called to see him should have made that obvious. However, since he has refused to co-operate, I'll sort this mess out the best way I can, and in doing so it will be to anyone's detriment to stand in my way, or cause confusion!'

Anako threw up his hands. 'D.C. vex!' he shouted.

'Me also!' Obieze rasped.

Bailey looked from the Chief to Hughes with bright eyes. Obieze looked over Hughes's head, his jaw set. As far as he was concerned the confrontation was over. Hughes on his part took Obieze in from head to toe with narrowed eyes, and turned on his heels. He commented as they were out of earshot, 'I greatly underestimated him in this instance. But we shall see what we shall see!' he added to Bailey as they got into the car. 'I've a feeling that we'll meet again, and this time on my own ground.' He motioned the driver to start the car.

Anako interposed. 'He bin tell me say, I be mark man.'

'Oh? Why didn't you tell me this before?'

'I bin tell Mr Underwood and Mr Jenkin, sir.'

'Oh yes, of course, I remember now, they did mention something of that nature to me.' Hughes sat thoughtfully for a minute. 'This isn't over yet,' he murmured to himself. Aloud he asked the interpreter, 'How's the painting going?' in an effort to distract from the worry which he knew Anako must have.

'We try, sir. It hard for get outside labour now because of farm work.'

'I see, well do the best you can.'

Anako nodded.

'We'll drop you off outside the gate, Mr. Anako. I won't come in this time, but in a week or so I'll send a relief to take temporary charge of the affairs here.'

'Yes, sir.'

'I want the painting finished by, or before, then.'

'Ah, it go finish, sir,' Anako assured him.

Hughes relaxed back in his seat. 'Excuse me, sir,' Bailey

E

M.B.C.—E

interrupted. 'D'you think the Chief had a hand in removing those stones?'

'I suspect he had. How else could they have vanished?'

'Children may have been responsible,' Bailey suggested.

'For removing all of them, with not one remaining? No, Bailey, this is more than a childish prank. It's adults' work, I would say. If children were the culprits, those stones wouldn't have completely disappeared from the road.'

'I don't understand you, sir.'

'Children would have kicked them about like a football, in which case the stones would've still been on the road, but away from where you and Bill originally placed them. They wouldn't have vanished completely, and the tyre marks . . . damnit!' cried Hughes slapping his forehead helplessly. 'I forgot to mention that while I was with him.'

'I gathered that those were completely swept away,' Bailey refreshed Hughes.

Hughes nodded. 'It goes back to what I said, that adults were responsible, and we don't have to look far to see who instructed them to do so.'

'But the afternoon that Bill and I were marking the road there was hardly a soul in sight until Mr Anako came along on his bicycle.'

'Have you had the opportunity . . . no of course, you wouldn't have. I've had the chance to sit in the Chief's lounge. A Chief's home stands on stilts and this isn't from idle whim, it's meant to. Sitting in the lounge you have the whole panoramic view of the town, every nook and cranny is spread before your very eyes. I wouldn't put it past Obieze that he quietly sat and observed you and Bill that afternoon, and that as soon as your backs were turned, he dispatched his thugs to erase everything you both did.'

When Bailey gasped at this, Hughes nodded. 'I wasn't too certain before, but I think I am now. That and the fact that Mr Anako here mentioned that he has a price hanging over his head!' Hughes leaned forward and asked the court interpreter, 'Which day did Obieze threaten you?'

'The same afternoon I pass Mr Underwood and Mr Bailey for my bicycle.'

'There you are,' said Hughes as he sat back with a satisfied smirk.

'What do we do now?' Bailey asked, shocked at what he had just heard.

'Do?' Hughes asked back. 'Nothing, at least not for the moment.' When he saw the horrified look on Bailey's face he enlarged. 'My dear Bailey, I'm a great believer in the old adage that if you give a man enough rope, he'll hang himself. We have to tread carefully or he'll make things very difficult for us. They're bad enough as they are. This is, after all, his territory. We're here to administer it of course, but that doesn't diminish the fact that it's his by right. These ancient kingdoms are an awful bind.'

As the native court, Ukana, came into view, Hughes roused himself. 'Here we are. This is where we leave you, Mr Anako, and don't worry. Get the place painted quickly. Everything else will fall in place at the right moment.'

'Yes, sir,' Anako replied as he got out of the car. He paused and saluted and the car pulled away.

Chapter Twelve

The offices of *The Daily Observer* drew people like a magnet. The editor, Michael Adiabua, for the sake of his lungs, had long given up his attempt to discourage casual callers and loiterers. The office steps were especially noted as a meeting place for the new and young intelligentsia. Here young men gathered every lunch hour, or when they could escape undetected from their dull office routine, to dissect every item of news in the paper, and argue out the hidden motive of what they thought to be a particularly evasive editorial.

The recent mine murder made it imperative that such a gathering should take place. A brief investigation outside by the editor showed an incredible scene. Young and old men in dull and bright robes thronged and crowded one upon another. Some were singing songs of lament, while others stood like prophets who, having instigated miracles, waited for them to happen. Yet others carried a forest of banners which read: ARMAGEDDON IS HERE. Another sign

read THE END OF THE WORLD IS NEAR, while another PREPARE
TO MEET THY DOOM.

Many just hung about curious, not knowing which way
to turn, which sign to read first, or whether to join in with
the singing. News flew fast, passing from mouth to mouth
until it grew out of proportion and was finally discarded.

In desperation the editor appealed that anyone not directly
concerned with the paper, or who had not come on business,
should leave the premises, but his plea fell on deaf ears. To
ask the police to disperse the throng would be inflicting a
severe wound on the very people the paper served as spokes-
man. So Adiabua and other members of his staff took
refuge behind closed doors in their offices. His news editor,
Martin Ofodile, was with him.

'I'd better have the fifteen pounds Godfrey asked for
before I forget,' he said to Adiabua.

'Is he really sure that something will come out of the meeting between him and this fellow?' Adiabua asked.

'He thinks so. However, let's not hold up his end of the
bargain.' Ofodile had barely finished speaking when a deaf-
ening roar came from the crowd. The two men ran to the
office balcony to find out what was taking place. There,
precipitated into the mob was Daniel Okoro, the chief news
vendor, the same man who had passed a free paper through
the window during the meeting of the town's council of
elders. Adiabua and Ofodile stared, shocked. When Adiabua
could speak he shouted, 'Look, leave that man alone or I'll
send for the police!' His threat seemed to penetrate and the
news vendor was let down gently. Adiabua beckoned to him
to come up and asked, when he joined them, 'What was the
matter, Daniel?'

'I no know, sir. They ask if I get any more paper to sell.
When I say paper finish, they pick me up for air.'

'Better stay here until things quieten down.'

'I think it right make I tell you now say, I see three mans
day before yesterday for road junction for evening near my
place. They put them head together and converse quiet.'

'Oh? Did you see their faces?' Ofodile asked him.

'Only small, small, sir, but if I see them again, I think I go
fit know them.'

'Have you seen the people before?' Ofodile went on.

'I think so but the whole thing hazy for my mind. I sure

I see them before, and at the same time, I no too sure. There be difference when you see people for evening-time when it begin for get dark small, small, and when you see them again for morning-time.'

'What's on your mind?' Ofodile asked.

'I think I talk to the three mans before, sir. When I waka waka go for my mistress, Evangelina place, for my chop, I say to myself, Daniel, I think you talk to the mans before, I think you know them.'

'What were they saying? Did you hear?' Ofodile continued.

The news vendor shook his head. 'Ah, that I no fit know. I sit for my verandah and it no too close to them, but they look as if they get some worry for them mind . . . er . . . how you say the word? Er . . . er.'

'Agitated?' Ofodile supplied and demonstrated.

'That be him, sir!' shouted the news vendor and carried on. 'The mans put them head close.'

'Can't you recall at all where you first saw the men?' inquired Ofodile. The news vendor thought for a while and shook his head sorrowfully. 'No, sir, I no fit put my finger for the place I see them before just now, but as I say, if I see them again, I go fit know them.'

'You can't guess at their names?' Ofodile pressed.

'Ah no, I no want for make mistake.'

'All right, you may wait in the newsroom until it's safe for you to go home,' Ofodile instructed him.

When the news vendor had left, Adiabua asked Ofodile, 'You showed unusual concern about the whole affair, why?'

'Because as I told you before, he's my informer. It was he who gave me the names of the six miners who are also staunch members of the secret society. Daniel doesn't get around merely because he's a vendor. There's nothing that happens here he doesn't get to hear about before it becomes generally known. If he's worried as well as suspicious about the men he saw chatting, then I'm sure that there's reason for his concern.'

'I see,' replied Adiabua. 'Well, I'll just sign a cash voucher for the fifteen pounds Godfrey requested.'

As the two went into the editor's office Ofodile began to pick up things and put them back again. Adiabua looked up from the voucher he was signing. 'What's the matter, Martin, you suddenly don't seem yourself,' he observed.

'Oh, I'm all right,' said Ofodile airily, 'but I've a hunch to take Daniel with me when meeting Godfrey tonight,' he said gravely.

'Why?' asked Adiabau, putting down his pen.

'Just a hunch, I can't explain it.' They stared at each other for seconds without blinking.

'You're not afraid are you? We can still call the whole thing off.'

'Don't mind me, but I'd much rather he came with me.'

'By all means, and take care.'

'I'll do that, and I'd better get hold of him before he escapes. I'll be back for the voucher,' he said, dashing out.

Hughes reached Utuka just a little after two. Underwood met him and Bailey as the two were going up the office stairs. It was past closing time but most of the officials had thought they had better hang on until the D.C. returned.

'We've just returned from a fruitless journey,' Hughes informed him.

'Oh?' replied Underwood.

Hughes looked at him surprised. 'Didn't Mark tell you that I went to Ukana this morning?'

'Yes, he did mention something about it,' replied Underwood and braced himself for what was coming next.

'Well, why are you behaving as though you knew nothing about it then?'

Bailey lowered his laughing eyes.

Underwood swallowed. 'It was the fruitless part that surprised me.'

'I dare say! Did you think I'd have him manacled and brought down with me?' he asked. When Underwood did not reply, Hughes went on, 'That sort of thing takes time and planning. Besides, I can't touch him, not without absolute proof. I suspect him, of course, of ordering his boys to remove the stones you and Bailey placed, but that's all. Men like him aren't arrested for doing such a thing, lesser men perhaps. But he's been warned. He's an educated man and understands me perfectly. And yet, and yet my mind tells me that there's something more besides the stones and the threat to the court interpreter. Something very serious has happened in Ukana, a van starting up in the night, tyre marks swept away, stones removed . . . and I cut down to size.'

Underwood and Bailey listened as Hughes rambled on. 'Whether he knows what's happened to Maurice, or where he is, I don't know. He told me he was sorry to hear about it. Oh God! I don't know. Of course, he's within his rights in refusing to come down and see me. The rulers here, I find, are always arrogant. The son isn't a patch on his late father though. That fellow always stood on his hind legs!' He sighed and asked Underwood, 'Still no news about Maurice?'

'None whatsoever.'

'I'd better yet again write and wire to the Governor, though what I shall say this time, frankly I don't know.'

'But it isn't your fault what's happened, sir,' said Bailey.

Hughes looked at Bailey's young and innocent face, open and trusting, the clear blue eyes free of all deception, and sighed. How wonderful it would be to be that age again, he thought. Aloud he told him, 'Whether it's my fault or not, the thing is, I'm responsible here. That I should lose or be totally unaware of the whereabouts of one of my men, isn't a very good recommendation. It doesn't say much for my ability to manage the affairs here, and heaven alone knows, I try to do my best. But explaining my efforts to the Governor in the present circumstances will not only be difficult, but will also be disbelieved!' He stood in the corridor as if reluctant to go into his office. 'This affair will finish me if I don't resolve it quickly. Before I left for Ukana this morning I was so confident that I'd have the problem solved. When you and Bailey told me about the tyre marks, then Jenkins and you, Bill subsequently told me they'd vanished, and the night-watchman talked about a van starting up in the night, I thought I had the whole thing sewn up. Until I confronted Obieze. From then on I was no longer sure, something seems to have gone wrong somewhere. The door seems to have been strangely shut in my face.'

'Perhaps you tried to act too hastily and jumped to a conclusion,' said Underwood.

'Conclusion?' asked Hughes, annoyed. 'My deductions were accurate, but the sum total of all the answers is wrong, which to a rational mind is ridiculous. I just don't know where I went wrong on leaving here this morning,' he wailed, beating his right fist into his left palm. 'Perhaps I expected to trap Obieze from the word go.'

'Maurice may still turn up, you know, and then it will be like the memorable meeting between Stanley and Livingstone!' Bailey said consolingly. Hughes grunted and Underwood could not help smiling at the incongruity of the comparison.

'There may never be a Maurice stretching out his hand for me to presume. That's what I'm afraid of,' Hughes replied quietly.

'I think you're being too hasty again . . .' Underwood started to say.

'No,' Hughes cut in. 'I think if I could get Obieze away from his home ground for an interview, I'd have more success. It's always been difficult to do business with them, or interview them, when they're surrounded by their retainers and hangers on. But how can I budge him?' he asked of no one in particular. 'Send Mark in, will you?' he said tiredly. 'I've just one more trump card to play and in the meantime I'll notify the Governor.'

Everyone started to speak at once as soon as Hughes and his party left. Obieze lifted his hands for silence and when all was quiet told them, 'I want make everybody go! I go send word for which day I want for see you.' Within minutes the audience chamber was empty, with the exception of two guards and the interpreter. He motioned them to follow him to his outer sanctum.

'What you think?' he asked of his men generally as he sat down. When they began to give their varying opinions all at once, he waved his hand to stop them. 'I no want for go deaf!' he informed them heatedly. 'I want to hear what you think, but not altogether. Make you tell me man by man.'

'I no think say D.C. finish yet, I think he go come back. I no think say, we reach end of matter,' his interpreter, Odibe, informed him.

Obieze sighed and turned to his two bodyguards. They both agreed with the interpreter. They stood back and looked on perplexed. They had never seen the Chief so agitated before. His interview with Hughes had left an after-effect, a climax of roaring uncontrolled rage. 'For which place be Okafor and Chukwuka!' Obieze shouted at last and wrung his hands.

His interpreter spoke up again with fitful breath, 'For them farm.'

This information annoyed Obieze even more as he had not yet been able to pay a visit to the workers tilling his farm. 'Go bring them come!' he said in a vindictive tone. 'This is no be time for farm!'

His aides, unwilling to witness any further rage, darted out from the sanctum and through the small wooden gate, in different directions. Obieze stared at their departing backs with unseeing eyes.

Chukwukka and Okafor were reclining in their hammocks without a care in the world when the Chief's aides arrived. Okafor looked up and asked the three new arrivals who suddenly stood before them, 'What be the matter now?'

Obieze's interpreter told him. 'Chief vex. I think he be inside trouble. D.C. come this morning-time for talk with Chief.'

Okafor and Chukwuka sat up. 'Eh?' they both asked at once.

When the interpreter nodded, Chukwuka asked, 'What D.C. want?'

'It be long story. I think it go be better if Chief tell you himself.'

'So Chief want for see we, eh?' Okafor asked as he put away his snuff container in his hold-all bag.

'That be reason why we come,' the interpreter assured him.

'Now-now?' asked Chukwuka looking for his fly wisk.

'Now-now,' Odibe, the interpreter, rejoined.

'All right,' replied Okafor and Chukwuka together as they jumped down from their hammocks.

Work had temporarily stopped as the workers stood up with their hoes trying to catch a word here or there on what brought the Chief's servants to the farm. Chukwuka, on whose farm the work was taking place this morning, ordered everyone to get back to work.

As the five walked a few yards away from the farm, Okafor asked, 'Anybody be with Chief?'

'No, Mr Okafor, Chief be by himself,' was the interpreter's reply. This information brought an exchange of glances between the two the Chief had sent out his aides to summon. They all walked now in silence until they reached Obieze's compound. The Chief's retainers stood aside, a slight knock, the door creaked and opened. The invited guests entered, the door creaked again and was shut.

The Chief watched the two men approach him, his eyes not leaving their faces. When the summoned men finally settled on small stools, Obieze cleared his throat and said stringently: 'D.C. come for here.' Okafor and Chukwuka said nothing. Obieze eyed them, swallowed and waited for this information to sink in. When this fact was established by the anxious tremors on the men's upper lips, Obieze went on, 'He come for ask who take rockery come out for road.' His listeners again made no reply, but the throbbing of their foreheads told Obieze that they were still with him, and were following every word he said. 'I think he get something else for mind for ask, but as he not get success about the rockery palaver, he no ask the other thing he get for mind to ask.'

'What he get for mind?' inquired Okafor, his senses alert.

Obieze smiled his contempt. 'About the real thing way happen to Mr Mason. He say since the man come here last week, say, he loss.'

Okafor and Chukwuka looked stunned.

'But I bin think say, that business finish,' Chukwuka murmured anxiously when he found his voice. 'I bin think we cover all the smell!'

Obieze nodded and sighed. 'So me also bin think. But it no look like say D.C. think the same thing we think.'

'What we go do now?' Okafor asked in a far-away voice.

Obieze took out his snuff container and tapped the lid. 'We go wait and see what D.C. do first. I no think make we show him our hand first,' he replied, gazing into space.

After a few seconds Okafor asked Obieze again, 'You think D.C. go come back?'

Obieze gathered his loin cloth securely about him. 'Who know? Me no know. Nobody know what white man think. They no tell anybody what be inside them mind. They just go for action! Ah, white man vex me!' he said bitterly.

Here Chukwuka thought he had better make his voice

heard as Okafor had been doing most of the talking with the Chief. 'D.C. no tell you he go come here today?'

Obieze gave a painful smile and slapped his thigh. 'No, he just come.' But he thought it only fair to enlighten the two men further about the events preceding the District Commissioner's visit. 'But he send word plenty time to me to go to Utuka to meet him, but I refuse.'

Okafor and Chukwuka were taken aback. 'But you for go,' said Okafor hastily after the initial shock.

'And make him catch me?' Obieze asked incredulously. When Okafor and Chukwuka kept quiet, he carried on, 'The D.C. no tell me what he want me for. I no fit go like small boy because he clap him hand!'

'But maybe what you think D.C. think, no be what the man think at all,' Chukwuka argued. 'And it no be for him mind,' he added.

'If it no be for him mind, what you think be for him mind, hmmm? How, he asked me about rockery?' Obieze countered.

'Rockery and kill people different,' Chukwuka told him.

'How?' Obieze snapped.

'So, we just wait for see, eh?' Okafor asked gently.

Obieze rubbed his eyes. 'Yes. What else for do?' he asked them helplessly. The three sat for a while in complete silence. 'I think make you go now,' Obieze told them. Chukwuka and Okafor got up and bowed out, but they could have saved themselves the trouble, for all the Chief noticed or cared.

'You asked to see me?'

'Yes, Mark, please sit down,' said Hughes. He took a deep breath. 'Well, I'm back from Ukana.'

'So I see,' Jenkins replied, holding his tongue further.

'Nothing happened.'

'I gathered that too.'

'The question is, what do I do next?' Hughes asked himself, looking up at the map of the British Isles on his office wall. He brought his attention back to Jenkins. 'I've one last effort in mind, but I don't want to use it except as a last resort.'

'The effort being ... ?'

'I haven't formulated it properly in my mind, but I will

139

in time. It's what to do in the meantime that I'd like to know.'

'It's still only Wednesday. Maurice has only been missing three days,' Jenkins pointed out, hoping that this fact would help to curb his senior officer's anxiety. But Jenkins's solicitous words were lost on Hughes who reminded him, 'Four on my calendar. I include last Sunday when I saw him drive to the club. Missing anyone here for four days is a serious thing.'

'I quite agree, George.'

'Well?' asked Hughes, hoping that Jenkins would come up with something.

Once bitten, twice shy, thought Jenkins and licked his lips. He said uncommittedly, 'Frankly I don't know, George. The whole thing is most worrying and confusing.'

Hughes, who had leaned forward eagerly awaiting the other man's ideas, now sat back disappointed when nothing was forthcoming. 'I should say it is,' he replied almost rudely. 'I'm writing the Governor today, but frankly I just don't know what to say.'

Jenkins looked at him sharply. 'The truth of course. The longer you delay in telling him, the worse it'll get.'

'I agree, but the truth, dear Mark, is sometimes the hardest thing to write.'

'In this instance it's plain, simple and straightforward.'

'Yes, it's just that. But I wish I didn't have to write the letter at all. I wish Maurice was here. I wish everything was calm and normal again,' said Hughes, almost pleading. He again looked at Jenkins as if hoping to get the answer from him. But when Jenkins remained mute, Hughes sighed and looked away. 'There's no easy answer, or alternative, is there?'

'No,' Jenkins replied softly, feeling sorry for the man for the first time since they had known each other.

'I'll be in my office a little longer than usual in case anyone wants to see me.'

'I don't know what I can do to help, George,' said Jenkins earnestly.

'It's most difficult,' Hughes replied wretchedly. 'However . . . oh, by the way, I'd be grateful if you'd tell the wives of our missing local staff about the situation.'

'I'll do that.'

'And, Mark,' Hughes called as Jenkins turned to leave. 'Use as much tact as possible. If what I suspect is true, and I mean suspect,' said Hughes, punctuating each word and looking at Jenkins steadily, 'I'll see they get a good settlement.'

Jenkins's hair stood up. 'You don't think . . .?' he asked gravely, unable to say the rest of the unpalatable words.

'I don't know. I just don't know.'

'Fifteen pounds all accounted for,' commented Ofodile, the news editor, as he put the money into an envelope.

'I rang the police, they'll have some of their men there,' Adiabua, the editor, told him. 'By the way, what time are you meeting Godfrey?'

'I want to be there at half past seven, he's seeing the man at eight.'

'I'd better let the police know about that too.'

'Good. Daniel, the news vendor, agreed to come with me.'

'Be careful, Martin,' Adiabua warned. 'I've nothing against martyrs, but I'm very fond of you!'

'With the police behind us?'

'That's what worries me. They may louse it up!'

'It's nice to know that if the inevitable happens, I'll be missed,' mocked Ofodile. They both laughed, then became serious again.

'I'll be here waiting,' said Adiabua soberly.

'Thank you.'

Chapter Thirteen

The world of the secret society is an entity in itself, and the people who lead it, as well as their members as a whole, are no different as far as appearances go, from the rest of us. There is only one exception. Whereas non-members are free and at ease with the world, the secret society members are inwardly ill at ease and at odds with most of what surrounds them. Understandably tight lipped about their mumbo-jumbo, they spring to action like a cornered animal if that mumbo-jumbo is ridiculed, or laid bare with serious intent. They have various ways of greeting one of their number – an intense stare, with eyes glittering, a slight twist of the wrist on meeting each other, a faint smile with the right corner of the mouth twitching. And as they have their mode of greeting, so too do they have signals for deciding the fate of an unsympathetic outsider. The swivelling of both eyes to the right in a set and impassive face, means that the use of juju to inflict illness, madness included of course, should seriously be considered. The face looking downwards for a second, and then brought dramatically upwards, accompanied by a deep breath, signifies that the enemy is to die. If the face continues to look down it means not yet, leave the unhappy man alone, at least for the time being.

It was to help Onyeso with the task of finding out the names of the society's hierarchy that Martin Ofodile and Daniel Okoro set out. They were there just before half past seven. Ofodile waited and then cleared his throat to make Onyeso aware that he had arrived. Onyeso in turn signalled back in the same manner and walked in the direction of the signal he had heard. They said nothing as the envelope containing the fifteen pounds changed hands, after which Onyeso went back to stand where the signpost signified the thirty mile limit.

Ofodile, his eyes accustomed to the darkness now, saw Onyeso clearly leaning against the signpost. There was a slight rustling of dead leaves near where Ofodile and Daniel Okoro stood. 'Police,' hissed a voice and Ofodile and Daniel shed ten years and sighed with relief.

The town of Amaku stood at a distance in complete darkness. The normal sight and sound of lorries approaching and leaving town were strangely absent, which Onyeso, Ofodile, and Daniel thought was unusual, until they realised that the police must have taken a hand in halting lorries about to leave town, at the lorry station where passengers embarked; also stopping those wanting to get into the township somewhere, ten or five miles out of town. It was an eerie night. Then all of a sudden, without warning and from out of no-where, came someone on a bicycle. He braked beside Onyeso.

'I told you I'd come,' said the man from the night before.

'So you said,' Onyeso conceded.

'Did you bring the money?'

'Yes. I have it on me.'

'Good. Let's have it.'

'Oh, no,' Onyeso replied, raising his voice a little so that his colleague from the *Observer*, as well as the police could hear. 'I want you to tell me first, the names of the members of the secret society.'

The man demurred. 'No one does business like that in this country, in this region. That isn't the way Africans do business. Africans take money first, and then give information,' he protested.

'I've a lot of money on me. The fifteen pounds we agreed on. I can't just hand them over to you like that,' said Onyeso snapping his fingers, 'and have you run away on your bicycle!'

'Don't you trust me?'

'I do. But a lot of money is a lot of money.'

'All right. Let me just have a look at the money to satisfy myself that you brought it with you.'

Onyeso poked the envelope slightly out from his right hand pocket. 'The money's inside the envelope,' he said.

The man changed his tune again. 'It's the money first, or no information!'

Onyeso felt cornered. He thought for a while. He certainly did not want to stand there all night arguing, at the same time he did not want the man to run out on him after he had given him the money. He thought of a happy medium. 'Look, I'll hold your bicycle while you count the money to see if it's correct. I want you to tell me the names of the members of the secret society as you count.'

'What sort of business is that?' inquired the man. 'How do you expect me to tell you their names as I count. I've only one mouth!'

'All right. I'll hold your bicycle as you count,' Onyeso proposed.

'And after that?' the man asked, laughter running through his voice.

'It doesn't matter. Here's the money,' said Onyeso, proffering the envelope as he remembered that Ofodile and the police were around somewhere. 'You can tell me the names after you've finished counting.'

The man chuckled. 'Now, you're talking sense,' he told Onyeso, stretching his hand out for the envelope. There was a pause punctuated by the crackling noise made by the red and white West African currency as it was being counted.

'Satisfied?' Onyeso asked when the man had finished.

'Indeed. You kept your promise,' the man replied, pocketing the money in his hip pocket.

'Well?' asked Onyeso.

'Well, what?' snarled the would-be informer.

Onyeso paused for a second to collect his senses. 'The names. That was our agreement. You can't have suddenly forgotten,' he told him in an anxious tone.

The man began a recitation that not only shocked Onyeso, but left him cold and trembling.

'I told you that nothing happens here – in this region – that I don't know about. Not a fly passes, and I don't know his destination. Not one lizard lays eggs, and I don't know when it will hatch! I am a member of the secret society! All that nonsense you told me about the place you work. Do you think I don't know?' he asked Onyeso icily, and went on, 'You are on the staff of *The Daily Observer*. You went to the Sunshine Bar to collect information for your paper!'

Onyeso stood rigid. The beating of his heart drummed in his ears.

'Well, what do you say now?' continued the man with glee. 'Am I right or wrong? *The Observer* wants to help the police to catch us,' he added frostily.

'Please give me back the money,' Onyeso said slowly.

His tormentor laughed. 'Is that all you can say? Is *The Daily Observer*'s money the only thing that's worrying you? Doesn't your life worry you at all? You will die tonight!'

There was no reply from Onyeso. His enemy carried on however, 'Some of the fifteen pounds will be given to Josiah Agba's widow. The rest will go to the secret society.'

'You had better come with us!' said a detective dramatically. So engrossed was Onyeso's tormentor that he didn't realise what was happening or who spoke to him. 'What is it?' he asked.

'I said you'd better come with us!' the detective repeated.

The man swung round and blinked. 'This wasn't in our bargain,' he hissed at Onyeso as he saw the officer.

'What you wanted to do to me wasn't in the bargain either,' Onyeso countered, relief nearly making his legs wobble.

Ofodile and Daniel Okoro now joined the detective and the other two. Daniel Okoro, the news vendor, nudged Ofodile. 'This be the man I see with other two men as they chat near my house, and I sit for verandah and watch them. I tell you and Mr Adiabua so this afternoon-time.'

'Are you sure?' Ofodile asked the news vendor.

'I sure!'

'You're under arrest,' said the detective to the secret society man.

'I beg your pardon? I've done nothing!' the man told the officer.

'Don't waste my time,' the detective told him. 'You're under arrest and charged with trying to obstruct the cause of justice.'

'What!' shouted the man, and then, 'You'll see!' he threatened the detective. 'You'll all see.' He clapped his hands and seven other men sprang from the bush.

At this the detective blew his whistle. A police van roared at breakneck speed towards them with its headlights full on. Several policemen were already running towards the scene on foot with their batons held high in the air. Others combed the bush around them with search-lights in case there were more secret society members lurking about.

'Jesu cry!' shouted the rounded-up secret society members in unison. In another minute they were all handcuffed and shoved into the police van. 'I believe you've something for me,' said Onyeso to his would-be murderer.

The stunned man looked at him uncomprehendingly. 'You've my fifteen pounds,' Onyeso repeated. Before the man could speak a constable wrenched the sum out of the arrested man's pocket and handed it over to Onyeso.

'Jump in, we'll give the three of you a lift into town,' the detective told the men from the *Observer*.

The van stopped at the main road outside the police station. The newspaper men got out first and quickly went into the station to await the arrival of the other eight men, who jumped out and paused, stricken with fear. What would happen to them? How long would they be held in there? Would they be able to come out again? How soon would the white hangman hang them?

Onyeso's would-be informer shook his head in despair and beat his chest with his free hand. When he made the bargain with the newspaper man inside the Sunshine Bar, he had not realised that it was on him, and not the other man, that the shadow of death would cross. He dropped his head sorrowfully.

Crunch, crunch, was the sound of the arrested men's footsteps on the gravel path, the measured march of men who had been arrested by the arm of the law. They came through the door of the police station and stood before the desk.

'I'm Detective Obindu,' said the man who had arrested them at the thirty mile limit sign out of town. 'This evening, with fifteen other policemen, I was on the main road leading in and out of town and I saw this man,' he said, pointing at Onyeso's man. He went on, 'And the other seven came out from behind the bush with the intent to kidnap and mutilate these three newspaper men over there, and myself included. The other police officers and myself took these eight men into custody. I arrested them and charged them with trying to obstruct the course of justice.'

The eight accused stood looking in different directions. Now inside the police station and having been formally charged, they seemed scarcely interested in the proceedings, but they were brought suddenly to attention when Sergeant Okwusili dipped his pen noisily in the ink well.

'What are your names?' he asked with his customary lisp.

'Augustine Egbu,' said Onyeso's tormentor. 'Fabian Ors ; Ben Ogu ; Friday Nze ; Paul Achotam ; Cyprain Anelo ; Francis Ochakanma ; Felix Ilo.'

There was silence and the scratching of the pen. 'And your addresses?'

4, Market Road! 103a, Burial Ground Road ; 16, Victoria Street ; 2, Expansion Road ; 65, Recreation Road ; 14, Hospital Road ; 54, Broad Street ; 6, St Agnes Crescent.'

'Your occupation?'

All replied in unison, 'Trader!'

Okwusili put down his pen. 'Search them,' he said, and the eight put up their arms while eight officers ran their hands through the men's pockets and placed what they found on the desk. There were penknives, old-fashioned razor blades, hammers and various home-made implements dessigned to inflict grievous harm.

'Lock them up separately,' said Okwusili.

Detective Obindu turned to Onyeso and his colleagues. 'You'll hear from us. We'll be calling on you again.' The *Observer* men left. The arrested men were taken away. As the key of the cell was about to be turned on Augustine Egbu, the tormentor of Onyeso, the man said, 'Look, I'm a very rich man. I'll give you ten pounds if you let me out!'

The officer's mouth hung open, he stared at the captive round eyed. He could do with ten pounds, he thought.

'All right, twenty pounds!' shouted the captive.

Still the officer said nothing, his mind on what he could do with twenty pounds.

'Thirty pounds!' the man pleaded, presuming that the officer's silence meant that a satisfactory sum acceptable to him had not been reached.

'Forty pounds!' the man proposed, wild eyed.

The officer licked his lips. Then he remembered suddenly who he was, and the duty he was charged to perform. 'Shut up!' he shouted back at the captive and turned the key quickly before temptation reared its head again.

'This is the strangest assignment I've been on,' commented Onyeso to his editor as they sat in the latter's office recounting the events of the evening.

'And the nearest you've been to death, I would imagine,' Adiabua told him.

'To be quite candid, on reflection, I rather enjoyed the feeling of having one foot in the abyss,' Onyeso told them. The editor, and the news editor also, stared at him. Onyeso burst out laughing as he saw the look of repugnance on their faces.

After the editor recovered from Onyeso's utterance, he asked: 'By the way, Godfrey, what's this about the D.O. missing? The story you phoned in?'

'The night-watchman in Ukana gave me the tip-off as I told Martin. I was there actually asking about the trouble between the D.O., his Assistant and the Chief.'

Adiabua looked up sharply. 'Oh? What about them?'

'The Director of Information told me that it's nothing more than the present Chief's father being buried with several heads. He was carpeted as a result by the two government officials.'

'No connection at all with the secret society?'

'I don't know. I wasn't there long enough to find out. I'll leave in the morning if you like to make further inquiries.'

Adiabua shook his head. 'No. Let's sit tight here and get on with the job at hand. We don't know how soon you'll be needed here by the police to give evidence.'

Chapter Fourteen

EIGHT MEN ARRESTED AND CHARGED, screamed the headline. The lead story went on to say:

'In an unprecedented swoop the police last night, following a tip off, arrested and charged eight men who are believed to be members of the secret society. The arrests took place on the main road leading in and out of town. All the men arrested are detained at the main police station until a date is set for a hearing.'

The story went on to list the names and occupations of the eight arrested.

'Well,' said Hughes. 'Events have certainly moved fast!'

Jenkins who was with Hughes in the latter's office for an entirely different matter asked, 'I wonder who tipped them off?'

'I don't know,' replied Hughes, 'but whoever did it should be congratulated.' He looked up from the paper. 'You've read it of course,' and without giving Jenkins a chance to reply continued, 'The list of names is staggering. To think that these men, in their quiet and vicious way, control the movements, promotions and what have you, in the mine. Any member from their rank and file can rise to the very top, not as a plexus of individual striving, but as a result of nepotic practices.'

'I suppose their motto is, if you belong, you're in, if you don't, you're out.'

'There's no other news in the paper except that,' added Hughes unnecessarily. 'I've been following the case closely.'

'Oh? Why?'

'I've my reasons.'

'Anything beyond the average reader's interest and concern?' Jenkins asked with the corners of his mouth twitching.

'They may have ambushed Maurice! If they can commit a senseless murder at the mine, there's nothing to stop them from killing a District Officer. That's why!' said Hughes.

'For heaven's sake, George, I doubt it. One minute you suspect Obieze and the next the secret society. What possible reason could they have in Maurice's case?'

'You never know, besides there's no law that says I should put all my eggs in one basket. However, we were discussing Arthur.'

'He's still away surveying. He only left two days ago, and according to you, he'll be away for a fortnight or so.'

Hughes frowned. 'I know it sounds silly, but I'm a little worried about Arthur being away. I know I should have thought about it before he left. I wouldn't have been so distressed were it not for Maurice's plight and the activities of the secret society, or whatever, it is they call themselves. However, I want action now instead of words. Phone all sub-stations except Ukana. Tell them to send their men out to scout their individual area.'

Jenkins raised his brows. 'Was this the plan you mentioned the other day that you had in mind?'

'No, this is an entirely new venture. I want no stone unturned first. My other plan I'll use as a last resort.'

'If you want Arthur back, we can always phone the rest house you know, his wife will most certainly be there.'

'Hmm. By the way, didn't you tell me that that reporter, I forget his name, asked you about the interview Maurice and MacIntosh had with the Chief?' asked Hughes, changing the subject.

'Yes. But that's normal for a newspaper man. He's the chief reporter for the whole region, but he covers this area in particular because the headquarters are here. Naturally he may've heard about the incident and purely wanted to know more.'

'He wasn't in court when it took place?'

'He may not have been. I don't know. From what I've heard the proceedings didn't take place in court but in MacIntosh's office.'

'Then how did he know that it took place at all?'

'What are you getting at?' Jenkins asked.

'I'm just pursuing a line of thought.'

Jenkins looked at him wonderingly. 'There's always a certain amount of commotion when the Chief appears in court, or anywhere else for that matter. Any one of the people hanging about the court that day may've told Godfrey.'

'And also informed him that Maurice was missing?'

'You think that Obieze may've leaked the story about the interview? And may also have done away with Maurice, and then told Godfrey to inquire and use both stories? And the blaze the story would cause would camouflage his part in it?' Jenkins asked cynically.

When Hughes agreed Jenkins said, 'But that's a bit far fetched. What reason could he have for doing that?'

'As you said, diverting suspicion from himself.'

Jenkins tried not to smile but couldn't help it.

Hughes went on, ignoring the other man's amused face. 'I can't help thinking that there's some connection between Maurice and Ukana.'

'Of course there is. He came back from there on trek only last Friday to take MacIntosh to hospital, and went back on Saturday to collect MacIntosh's U.K. suit. And you suspect him of creeping back there on Sunday afternoon as he may've forgotten to lock the place up as you told him to. However, that's irrelevant now. Why not wait until I've phoned your instructions and the results are in? If they're negative, and you still think Obieze had a hand in Maurice's disappearance, and again I doubt this, then we can do something about it. But quite frankly, the idea's preposterous.'

When Hughes looked at Jenkins in a way that made the latter feel uncomfortable, Jenkins decided to be pleasant. 'All right, Obieze may've told Godfrey about the interview purely to show us in a bad light. But as regards the other thing, the last thing he'd do, if he did so at all, would be to inform the newspaper. People don't commit murder and then go around blabbing their crime to newspapers. Besides, he couldn't have done what you suspect him of doing, the man's literate.'

'The massacre of 1914 to 1918 wasn't done by illiterates!' Hughes replied dryly. 'However, far be it from me to try and find a scapegoat hastily.'

'Why didn't you ask him when you saw him yesterday?'

'Ask him?' Hughes said, surprised. 'My dear Mark, you're losing your touch in diplomacy. I may be jumping to a conclusion hastily, I don't know. I've never lost a man under me before, and it's gnawing at me terribly. I only hope it doesn't drive me round the bend. To me the way things are at the moment, every man's a suspect and every action suspicious.'

'There're a thousand and one places Maurice could be now. There are lots of villages around.'

'You put it so simply. Well, which one of the villages could he be in?'

'That I can't rightly say,' Jenkins admitted.

'Then we're back to square one,' said Hughes, leaning back in his chair and rubbing his eyes. 'Mark, send another message from me to Obieze, a sort of invitation this time. Tell him the Governor has just arrived unexpectedly on a two days visit and has asked him to come down, as he can't come up, as his time is limited. Tell him His Excellency wishes to confer a knighthood on him. Also tell him that I especially asked him to forget our last squabble in the light of the honour coming his way. We'll send a car up in the morning for him.'

Jenkins stared open-mouthed, speechless.

'Mark, please close your mouth. It's very unbecoming, particularly on a man,' Hughes told him quietly.

'You know that's not true, the knighthood and the Governor, I mean,' Jenkins said when he had gathered his wits.

'I know it isn't true, but I'm using both excuses as straws to break the camel's back. His father, until his dying day, still smarted from being passed over when Chief Ututu of Endebu Region, who Obieze II considered not his equal, was given a knighthood. This happened after Obieze and I were locked in a dispute on whether a road should go along the edge, but he thought cross, his favourite farming land. Obieze won, but I withheld from him what would've been the spoils of war, had the outcome been different, and instead gave it to the more congenial Ututu. Obieze, if I remember correctly, received an O.B.E. Nothing hurt him more than that gratuitous thrust. At one stage in the dispute the man actually accused me of trying to appropriate his land! I never forgot it, and I never forgave him!'

'And you think his son will come running?'

'I hope so. Son succeeding where his father failed, what? It's my last trump card.'

'I see.'

'Please phone the instruction to the sub-stations and this invitation to Ukana as quickly as possible.' Hughes paused, and then went on: 'By the way, I want to go on a little journey,' he said darkly.

'To where?' asked Jenkins.

'None of your business.'

Jenkins stood up to leave but Hughes did not look at him. Instead he was suddenly absorbed in a paper clip on his desk. What will he think of next, what will he do? thought Jenkins, as he tiptoed out.

The town of Amaku was still, as if a curfew had been imposed. No one, if they spoke at all, did so above a whisper. The streets of this normally busy town were virtually deserted, the few shops that opened, closed before lunchtime. Only in the offices of *The Daily Observer* was there life, with people speaking in their normal voices.

'We didn't think of getting pictures of the arrested men last night,' Ofodile, the news editor, complained.

'It doesn't matter, we'll do so when the trial begins. Anyway, in the situation the three of you were in yesterday, taking pictures was the least of my worries,' Adiabua told him. 'In the meantime, get the editorial staff together for a conference to see what we can scratch up for tomorrow's paper.'

Jenkins knocked and entered Hughes's office with the excitement the District Commissioner had never seen in his Director of Information before. 'I sent and received an answer from Chief Obieze – he'll be happy to come!'

'What, that was quick! Are you sure?' Hughes asked all in the same breath.

'That's what our man in Ukana, who personally took the message to him, phoned back to say.'

'Are you sure he's certain? Are you sure you got his answer right?' Hughes asked again, astonished.

'Do you want to ring him up yourself and check? There's nothing wrong with my ear drum! The answer I just gave you was what came through the line.'

'I'm very surprised,' Hughes murmured.

Jenkins looked abashed. 'But surely that's the reply you hoped for?'

'Most certainly, still, it's a little staggering. I didn't think, even though I hoped, the fish would bite the first time. I suppose, flushed with surprise, he didn't think it over, and let's hope he won't.'

Jenkins continued excitedly, 'I also phoned the other sub-stations, but I seriously doubt if it'll come to anything.'

'So do I, but it was just an idea.'

'Shall I ring them and tell them to call it off?'

'No, let them carry on. It's time they earned their fat pay packets.' He glanced at his watch. 'It's nearly two. I'm looking forward not only to my little journey, but to my lunch, to my dinner and to my bed as well.'

Obieze looked at his favourite wife in wonder after dispatching his reply to Hughes. 'I no know say, King George like me. He bin no like my father. I no know say, they even know me for England!'

His wife eyed him. 'You be big man. If you no know that, who go know?'

'Ah, Iru, the news make my heart glad! Even Hughes beg me to forgive him about all the nonsense he come here talk yesterday. I forgive him. I be Christian! Jesu cry! Tomorrow, before afternoon-time, I go be His Highness, Sir Edward Obidiegwu Obieze III. I no fit believe it! The thing no sink in yet. I no even be Chief for long time and I get this present from King George.'

His wife, watching him from the side line, thought, it need only take good news to bring out the ego and the little boy in every man. But as for Obieze, what his wife thought of him at this moment was like water on a duck's back. He boomed out, 'I want go sleep early today. Send that bugger, my interpreter, for go tell Okafor and Chukwuka say, palava with D.C. finish. Say, everything all right now!'

Iru darted out.

Husband and wife woke the following morning and prepared for their journey. Before they finished their breakfast of roasted yam with palm oil into which hot ground pepper had been poured, a car arrived and stopped outside the massive gate. Hughes's driver at the wheel, had had his instructions. Within ten minutes the driver switched on the ignition and the car moved on. Obieze waved to a crowd of onlookers and he and his wife settled back on the red upholstered seat and exchanged glances. They briefly entwined their hands. As the car neared Ujo River, Obieze turned his head and looked out from the car's rear window. As he did so it seemed to him that the red hills of Ukana quivered and loomed more gigantic and dangerous than he had ever seen them before. He shuddered and took his eyes away. He leaned back in his seat once more, this time his forehead was massed with sweat.

'Iru,' he called to his wife after some time and in a strange voice. 'Something I dream about last night. It no worry me before, and I forget about the dream because we glad and hurry too much this morning-time, because of the present King George say make Governor give me. But now, as I see Ukana hill, and ride inside this foreign motor car, the dream come back, and it worry me now.'

'Eh?' Iru turned slightly towards him to inquire.

He went on in the same strange voice as if she hadn't spoken. 'I dream, say, plenty birds hang and sing for all the branches of big obeche tree. Above the big branches, fly vultures. They fly round and round for sky. Then the big obeche tree fall beside Ukana hill, and all the birds, hundreds and hundreds, no know for which place for fly go. They fly this way, they fly that way.' He paused and looked at his wife and she saw the shadow of death cross his face.

'Iru,' Obieze went on, 'I be the obeche tree, way fall. The birds who, way, no know for which direction to fly, be the people of Ukana. The vultures way fly in the sky, fly because they wait for chop my carcass! I no think say, Governor come to Utuka. I no think say, King George give him medal to give me. And I no think say, they know me in England!'

154

He leaned forward and ordered the driver to turn back and return him and his wife to Ukana. His order fell on deaf ears. The driver braced himself, accelerated and kept his eyes on the road towards the destination where he had received his instructions.

If there was a glimmer of doubt about the dream in Obieze's mind before, there was none now. Whatever else he was, he was no coward when he had to deal with the tangible. It was when faced with the intangible that he appeared weak. He sucked in his breath, gathered his flowing loin cloth more tightly about him, and reached for his double-barrel. Avoiding the look of horror on his wife's face, he placed the twin opening of the gun in his mouth and fired.

Hughes was in his office talking with Jenkins when the driver burst in to tell him. They sat, stunned for a second.

'How could he have known? Who could've told him?' Jenkins asked after the driver had left with fresh instructions from Hughes.

'Mr dear Mark,' Hughes said, after he got some measure of control on his emotions. 'In each of us there's a still, small voice.' He stopped and added, 'I only wanted to interrogate him and not for what he just did to himself. When I first asked him to come down it was a call for help, nothing more. Had he come then, we'd probably have written Maurice off and this wouldn't have happened. But no, he chose to be stubborn, and not only that, he sent his men to remove the stones and wipe the road clean. When he did that my suspicion deepened. The debt has now been paid in full.'

'It certainly has been an eventful week,' Jenkins observed.

Hughes got up, walked to the window and stood looking at the shanty that was Utuka. With his back to Jenkins he said, 'Before we do anything else, ring that newspaper friend of yours, will you? I promised him that I'd keep in touch.'

'D'you mean Godfrey?'

'No, the other fellow. I forget his name.'

'I've no other friend there except perhaps his editor, Michael Adiabua, whom I've met only ...'

'That's him!'

'But I thought you never liked him, in fact you detested their whole set up!'

Hughes turned from the window. 'Now whatever gave you that idea?' he asked blandly.

Jenkins suppressed the protest that came to his lips. Instead he asked, 'What d'you propose to tell him?'

'About Maurice, and about Obieze being at the head of the secret society. He it was who instigated the murder of the murdered man's father as Obieze wanted to put up his own man as foreman of the mine. I also gather, that Obieze was responsible for the recent murder, as the murdered man knew too much. I'm sure they'd have used Obieze's connection with the murders had they known. Newspaper people don't get frightened easily. I got the story about who was behind the murders from my informer when I went on that little journey I mentioned to you yesterday. It wasn't easy. The man nearly jumped out of his skin as he told me. But with the huge sum of ten shillings dangling before his eyes, and the promise of protection, for what it's worth, thrown in, that seemed to reassure him.'

Jenkins looked on, speechless with admiration.

Hughes reached for the phone himself. 'What's his name again?'

'Michael Adiabua.'

'And his number?'

'Amaku 57.'

'I'll give him a story that will not only make his hair stand on end, but will send the sale of his scandal sheets soaring to unbelievable heights!'

Fontana African Novels

The Wanderers   Ezekiel Mphahlele
'Skilled and varied . . . a panoramic view of white and black Africa, full of perception.' *Times Literary Supplement.* 'Some novels tell one more, through fiction, than fact can ever do. *The Wanderers* is a book of this kind . . .' *Daily Telegraph*

The Naked Gods   Chukwuemeka Ike
'Brilliant . . . funnily entertaining . . . conflicts in a university campus, with sex, juju and witchcraft thrown in for good measure.'   *Birmingham Post*

Toads for Supper   Chukwuemeka Ike
'Scores a bulls-eye for Nigerian writing.'   *Guardian.* 'Charmingly funny, touching yet sad . . . executed with vivacity and deftness.'   *Sunday Telegraph*

Danda   Nkem Nwankwo
An Eastern Nigerian playboy, unashamedly in love with the good life.' 'A delight.'   *Times Literary Supplement.* 'Has a real comic touch.'   *Observer*

The Interpreters   Wole Soyinka
A novel of Nigeria today—from university common-rooms to society nightclubs to evangelical cults. 'A great steaming marsh of a book . . . brimful of promise and life.'   *New Statesman*

Voices of Africa *Edited by Barbara Nolen*
More Voices of Africa   *Edited by Barbara Nolen*
Stories, poetry and drama from yesterday and today—by by some of modern Africa's most famous authors.

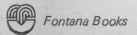 *Fontana Books*

Fontana African Novels

The Voice   Gabriel Okara
A lyrical, poetic and tragic story of the clash between a young, thinking Nigerian and the blind prejudices of his elders. 'One of the most memorable novels to have come out of Nigeria.'
Margaret Laurence

A Dream of Africa   Camara Laye
'Gently lays bare the soul of a young Guinean student in Paris returning home to the enveloping tribal pattern . . . A proud, poetic, visionary story.'   *Irish Times*

The Radiance of the King   Camara Laye
'A strange and beautiful book . . . The hero is a white man, called Clarence, who seeks to enter the service of a great, mysterious African king and travels far and suffers much to fulfil his desire. The book has a sparkling freshness; it is genuinely and deeply poetic.'   *Evening News*

The African Child   Camara Laye
The story of the author's childhood among the Malinke tribe. 'A remarkable book. Camara Laye is an artist and has written a book which is a work of art.'   *Times Literary Supplement*

The Gab Boys   Cameron Duodu
'Mr. Duodu lets off shafts at Civil Service corruption, the inadequacies of education, and the absurdities of British life as seen by Africans. The total effect is distinctly entertaining.'
Sunday Times

 Fontana Books

Fontana Russian Novels

The First Circle   Alexander Solzhenitsyn
The unforgettable novel of Stalin's post-war Terror. 'The greatest novel of the 20th Century.' *Spectator*. 'An unqualified masterpiece—this immense epic of the dark side of Soviet life.' *Observer*. 'At once classic and contemporary . . . future generations will read it with wonder and awe.' *New York Times*

Doctor Zhivago   Boris Pasternak
The world-famous novel of life in Russia during and after the Revolution. '*Dr. Zhivago* will, I believe, come to stand as one of the great events of man's literary and moral history.' *New Yorker*. 'One of the most profound descriptions of love in the whole range of modern literature.' *Encounter*

The Master and Margarita   Mikhail Bulgakov
'The fantastic scenes are done with terrific verve and the nonsense is sometimes reminiscent of Lewis Carroll . . . on another level, Bulgakov's intentions are mystically serious. You need not catch them all to appreciate his great imaginative power and ingenuity.' *Sunday Times*. 'A grim and beautiful tale . . . just as you think the whole thing is a very funny satire, a chilling wind out of the Ingemar Bergman country blows, and, yet again, as you search for some moral significance, there are pages of sheer and beautiful fantasy.' *Times Educational Supplement*

The White Guard   Mikhail Bulgakov
'A powerful reverie . . . the city is so vivid to the eye that it is the real hero of the book.' *V. S. Pritchett, New Statesman*. 'Set in Kiev in 1918 . . . the tumultuous atmosphere of the Ukranian capital in revolution and civil war is brilliantly evoked.' *Daily Telegraph*. 'A beautiful novel.' *The Listener*

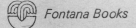 *Fontana Books*

Fontana Books

Fontana is best known as one of the leading paperback publishers of popular fiction and non-fiction. It also includes an outstanding, and expanding, section of books on history, natural history, religion and social sciences.

Most of the fiction authors need no introduction. They include Agatha Christie, Hammond Innes, Alistair MacLean, Catherine Gaskin, Victoria Holt and Lucy Walker. Desmond Bagley and Maureen Peters are among the relative newcomers.

The non-fiction list features a superb collection of animal books by such favourites as Gerald Durrell and Joy Adamson.

All Fontana books are available at your bookshop or newsagent; or can be ordered direct. Just fill in the form below and list the titles you want.

FONTANA BOOKS, Cash Sales Department, G.P.O. Box 29, Douglas, Isle of Man, British Isles. Please send purchase price plus 6p per book. Customers outside the U.K. send purchase price plus 7p per book. Cheque, postal or money order. No currency.

NAME (Block letters)

_____

ADDRESS

_____

_____

_____